A Great Retirement

Original story, cover illustration and novella by

Dr. Jed Griswold

Technical Advisor

Dr. Frank C. Griswold

ISBN: 979-8-9866137-5-8 (paperback)

ISBN: 979-8-9866137-6-5 (Kindle)

NOTE: The author, Jed Griswold, was once cast by Robert Casey in a stage play in Boston in the late 1990s. He is placed here in a 'cameo role' in this fictional work as a 'thank you' to Mr. Casey for that opportunity, and also because there is an age group of readers who will remember that radio/TV role, and who will appreciate that memory.

ACKNOWLEDGMENTS

Many thanks to my brother, Dr. Frank C. Griswold, for being even more than a good brother – a good inspiration for many of the funny and chaotic scenes in this novella, even though his own retirement stories in both an RV and an over-55 community have been, thankfully, much calmer.

And many thanks, as well, to my parents, Rev. Dr. Walter and Louise Griswold, for starting our ongoing family tradition of sharing the reading of *'Twas the Night Before Christmas.*

While most of the events in this story are fictional, the ability of the main characters to endure them is a hopeful reality.

ALSO BY THIS AUTHOR

The Power of Storytelling, Wood Lake Publishing.
Who Haunts This House, Griswold Consulting.
The Mysterious Old Woman, Griswold Consulting.

TABLE of CONTENTS

JED GRISWOLD

Griswold
Consulting

info @ griswoldconsulting.net

A Great Retirement

Chapter 1 – "You're fired!"

It was a typical day at a typical job with a typical assignment: entering data. "123, 72, 86, 12, 18, 34 – oh, wait, **33**, 34."

Franklin sighed as he looked at the unfinished stack of papers waiting to be processed and then he checked his watch. The inevitable "hour of boredom" had arrived, just after lunch, with his empty sandwich bag on top of scattered papers. His eyelids were heavy enough to lull him into a semi-nap, as he swiveled his chair to the clear but frost-covered window overlooking a lightly snow covered pine tree. It was a wintry December day in 2018.

Thinking to himself, in his half-awake state, "If only I could take a *long* vacation -- like the vacations I enjoyed so much in the past." He looked at the corner of his paper-filled desktop to view a specially framed photo. It was a montage of vacation scenes with his family, visiting national parks with well recognized monuments, recreation parks with twisting roller coasters, and quiet picnics under beautifully arching trees. Everyone, including the children, were having so much fun – and were equally so much younger.

Then a loud voice startled Franklin out of his half-dream. It was his annoying, no-nonsense boss, Mr.

Wilson. He was yelling from outside, a declaration of his imminent entry into the office.

"Franklin! Franklin!"

Coming out of his dream and back into the real world as though receiving a splash of cold water, he managed to respond, "Yes, Mr. Wilson?" "Franklin! Are you finished with the Lansbury file yet? They're coming for it in 5 minutes!"

Franklin rifled through the papers on his desk and answered in a hopeful tone, "Oh, yes, Mr. Wilson. I have it…..right….here…" But his immediate search was in vain.

Mr. Wilson entered the office, looking quite angry. "Well? Where is it? You know the Lansbury firm is our largest client! I promised those papers would be finished **today**!"

"It's almost finished, sir. It's here, somewhere…I can have it first thing in the morning."

Mr. Wilson took one look at the desk, and recognized Franklin's long-term state of disorganization: papers in uneven stacks with post-it notes on nearly every document. Then a glance at the filing cabinets along the walls confirmed his impression. All had half-opened drawers and file folders with papers sticking out of every one. His conclusion: "Franklin, you are the most worthless, inept, incompetent, moronic, lazy, disorganized, idiot who has ever worked for this company!"

Franklin could only muster a meek apology. "Mr. Wilson, I have been a loyal employee for *Wilson, Wilson, and Wilson, Incorporated* since your grandfather hired me, 38 years ago. I was his first hire, and for three generations, I have worked my fingers to the bone, on *this* very calculator." "Well, Franklin, that may be 38 years too many, because this time you have convinced me that you are a complete and utter failure as a human being. Do you hear me? **A failure!** The biggest failure the human race has ever seen!"

After a beat, Franklin realized it was time to muster up more; it was time to draw a line. He now stood taller and demonstrated an unusual backbone of strength as he assertively stated, "Mr. Wilson, I have listened, with patience, to 38 years of insults and humiliations from you, your father and your grandfather. It's time a man has to do what he has to do -- to stand up for dignity and self-respect. I will not tolerate your humiliation, belittling and disrespect. I AM A HUMAN BEING! I QUIT!"

"You can't quit, Franklin," came the response, but Franklin wasn't accepting this and he kept on, riding upon his momentum toward a final position.

"There comes a time when a man has to take a stand, with maturity and human dignity! So I repeat -- with maturity and human dignity -- I QUIT!"

"You can't quit, Franklin – because YOU'RE FIRED!" came *Mr. Wilson's* final declaration. "And per your contract from 38 years ago, any employee who is fired is not eligible for ANY form of severance pay! Pack your things and leave! Now!"

Mr. Wilson turned toward the door, then after a beat, turned back to Franklin. "Oh, and Merry Christmas!"

Breaking down in tears and crying like a baby, Franklin slumped to his knees, sobbing at Mr. Wilson's feet as his boss left the office with his now-former employee clinging to his ankles, all the way to the exit. Once left alone at the doorway, Franklin slowly stood, with difficulty, holding his back because of arthritic back pain, and he began to pack items from his desk drawer into his lunch paper bag. Then he walked toward the office door and exited with a look back at his desk.

Chapter 2 – *Movie Night*

Later that night, Franklin and Denise were seated at
the dining room table in their modest home sharing
a modest meal. They ate in silence. Though
Franklin was a strong extravert, speaking up often
and quickly, he was too embarrassed to speak of his
earlier experience at the office, and Denise, an
introvert, was too uncomfortable to bring up the
subject.

Denise took a bite of food then started to say
something as though she had a brilliant comment to
make, but she filtered her thoughts before making a
sound, and she returned to eating, silently.
Then...

"We'll make it, somehow. You can find another job
and I still have *my* job. Don't worry, Franklin."
Then, after hearing no response, she added, "Have
you called Daniel or Myra?"

Not really listening, Franklin was silently replaying
the day in his brain, nodding his head back and
forth and gesturing as though he were confronting
Mr. Wilson, and at the same time weighing the
events of the earlier scene, but all silently.
Franklin was naturally a verbal teletype, expressing
his thoughts and emotions with little prompt, but
tonight he was keeping his thoughts to himself. In
this moment of crisis, he was more inward and

silent, not prepared to verbalize his emotions, the very opposite of common extravert actions. But this time, the stakes were very high, and high stakes can change normal behaviors.

Looking at her watch, Denise spoke up. "Franklin, I almost forgot. It's our 'Movie Night' and the *Family Movie Hour* begins in five minutes," adding, "We need a distraction, especially tonight. I'll get the popcorn bag, you turn on the TV."

Dutifully but still silently, Franklin entered their small living room to turn on the TV. The movie was already playing in the background, but Franklin and Denise were not really watching. Then, true to his usual extrovert-like non-filtering before speaking, Franklin began to share his thoughts. "Remember when we were younger, and the kids where small, those wonderful family vacations we enjoyed?" Always the optimist, Denise joined in the over-simplified memory even though she knew that those vacations were sometimes wrought with disasters. "Oh, my yes. They were all such restful, educational vacations! We always came home refreshed and energized for returning to work, and the kids returning to school."

"Now the kids are all grown and those days are gone forever," lamented Franklin. And then a moment of genius struck. "But wait! I have an idea. You know what we need: another vacation, but this time, just for *us*. Just you and me, like our honeymoon, all over again.

Throwing a dash of cold water on the notion, "Oh, that's a great dream, Franklin, but how could we ever be able to afford that? You'll need to find another job and I'll have to keep my job, *forever.* We can't just *drive off into the sunset*!"

Then while seeming to stare into empty space, Franklin and Denise noticed an ad on TV – an ad which grabbed their and attention – and pulled at their dream.

"Did you ever think, 'I could never afford to retire and travel'? Well, have I got news for you! Not only can you afford to retire, you can afford to retire *and* travel *and* stay at home at the same time by taking advantage of our annual New Year's Special Sale!"

Now both Franklin and Denise were drawn in. "Last year's models are now deeply discounted to make room for this year's new models, and with our in-house financing, you can afford the RV of your dreams – with enough room and luxury to make it your permanent home! No more property taxes, water bills, yard maintenance. Just sell your house and *drive off into the sunset* in your new, home on wheels!"

Franklin and Denise looked at each other as if this was a message from an angel, just for them! The screen displayed a contact phone number and the two them bumped into each other scrambling to find paper and pen to write it down, which they were able to complete just in time. Franklin got to the phone first.

"I am responding to your ad about the annual New Year's Special Sale. Could we stop by in the morning to see what you have in stock? 10 AM? That would be fine. Yes, I'm Franklin Great. I'll see you then, Mr., uh --- yes, Mr. Withrow." Then he turned to his loyal wife, "Denise. Since this is going to be our second honeymoon," then getting on his left knee, "will you...'*drive off into the sunset*' with me?"

Denise smiled and looked lovingly into his eyes, dreaming of their next journey together. She responded without hesitation, "Yes, my dear, Oh yes!" Franklin responded, "You know, Denise - this could be more than a second honeymoon. This could be our *dream retirement*!" He stood tall and hugged Denise like he had when he first proposed.

Chapter 3 – The RV deal of the century

At precisely 10:00 the next morning, Franklin and Denise arrived at a door with the overhead banner reading, "*The Perpetual Vacation* RV Sales Center." By 10:04, they entered a large showroom which had a variety of recreational vehicles of every dimension -- small, medium and large. They looked at a smaller converted truck model and carefully checked the price sticker and they give each other a "we can afford that" look. But then, Franklin's eyes caught a glimpse of a super-fancy and very large model and his face lit up like a neon sign as he saw the "Super Discount" tag on the windshield.

The sales agent, Mr. Withrow, was observing all of this before approaching the Greats. "Mr. Great?" "Yes," came the response, which sounded like it was uttered under hypnosis.

"I'm Jim Withrow. Welcome to your next adventure!" "Well, I wouldn't jump to a conclusion too quickly, Mr. Withrow," replied Franklin, in a serious tone. "You see, I am a very cautious, conservative consumer, and I always research the data on any purchase, and I **never** make a major purchase on impulse."

At precisely 10:19, Franklin had signed a purchase contract at Mr. Withrow's desk. "Now, Mr.

Great…" which invited a casual reply, "Franklin…"
"Well, I want to congratulate you, *Franklin*, on
quite a savings on this purchase." Franklin smiled
from ear to ear.

Mr. Withrow continued, "Since you *are* a very
conservative and cautious consumer, I'm sure you
will want to protect your new home-on-wheels with
a *premium* insurance policy that covers absolutely
everything that could need repair. Being a very
savvy consumer, you know that it's normal for little
things to go wrong, and that little things over a
lifetime of retirement can, well, add up."
After only a brief pause, "It covers
EVERYTHING?"

The salesman continued, "Absolutely everything.
The dishwasher, the oven, the transmission, the
automatic slide-outs, even the tires!"

"Even the *tires*!" Franklin looked at Denise with
great pride.

"Oh, and even more! Let me give you an example of
the total coverage. We had a customer just last week
whose RV ran out of fuel right on a train track."
Franklin grimaced at the mental image, but Mr.
Withrow continued. "The owner had just enough
time to get out of the way before a high speed
freight train ran right into it and smashed it into
dust. Everything was covered and paid for with *no*

deductible! You're in luck, my friend. We are the *only* RV Sales company in the nation that offers this kind of premium insurance."

He handed Franklin the policy, with its price tag, to which his customer looked with shock at the cost. "Well, for **this** price, it's no wonder!"

"But, Mr. Great – ah, Franklin – you saved enough on the RV discount to cover the full premium. And if you pay a full 25 year coverage *today*, you will get *another* discount."

Thinking it over out loud true to his extravert trait, he repeated what had already been said, though in a slow summary, as though it were sinking in, "Everything...is...covered."

"Everything!"

Denise, after silently listening to the conversation in true introvert fashion, finally spoke up. "Franklin, don't you think it would be good to get input from Daniel or Myra?"

His first response showed on his face – a look of worry and a little frustration. But he quickly shifted gears with, "Let's do it! After all, retirement only happens once!"

Franklin signed the insurance contract and a smiling Mr. Withrow led them back into the showroom to the newly sold luxury RV. Franklin stopped to bow before it, much to Denise's embarrassment. But it only encouraged Mr. Withrow to begin his tour.

"Now let me review some of the special features of the model you just – very wisely -- purchased." They stepped into the RV. "Notice the expansive yet compact storage in these overhead cabinets. Now in an ordinary RV, if you were searching for something, you would have to manually open each cabinet, one at a time, to see what was inside that cabinet. That creates 2 problems." He walked down the aisle, to demonstrate his pitch. "One, it slows down a search, having to go one cabinet at a time, opening each one separately. Two, the doors open upward and since each door has to be manually closed, that makes for a hard stretch for someone shorter to reach up and close each door," nodding toward Denise, who was enough shorter than Franklin to make his point. "So our engineers created a one-button switch which opens *all* the cabinet doors at once. Another push of the same switch *closes* all the doors at the same time, saving both time and effort. This *green* button does all the work for you." He demonstrated each step.

"And most RVs these days have only a convection/microwave, but we know that many families in their retirement years appreciate an *old fashioned oven* for home baking and roasting *old-fashioned meals*. So we have that oven right here, below the microwave. And here's one more special feature, for those with minor back problems, since we know that many of our RVers tend to develop arthritis in their retirement." Mr. Withrow was a skilled salesmen; he had been very observant of Franklin's gait upon entering the salesroom, and it hit the target as the comment resonated with Franklin.

"With a push of this *blue* button…" he demonstrated the action, "…the oven door opens by itself. No more bending over to open the door!" Denise and Franklin were already smiling with pride about their new purchase.

"And, there's more," as the tour continued to the back of the RV. "The bedroom has a King size bed, with large closets for extra storage. And the breaker box is located here, in the bedroom, in case you have any electrical problems – which, of course, would be very rare. But if something major goes wrong, *this* breaker switch here, labelled **Emergency Shut-Off**, shuts *everything* down, until an electrician can safely start things back up – another safety feature."

But the tour was not yet finished. "Now, with our pneumatic system, with the high pressure lines hidden in the walls, you can also open the sliding bedroom door with a push of *this* button," as Mr. Withrow points to an *orange* button. Then as an aside, "Just don't nail anything into the walls, because if you hit one of those pneumatic lines, the bedroom door will automatically close and not be able to be opened again without a service call. Of course, a savvy consumer like yourself, would already know that." After Franklin's quick and expressive nod of agreement even though the information was all new to him, the sales pitch continued.

"And there's still more. This particular model has not one, not two, but *three* hydraulically-controlled slide-outs which expand the interior. There is one in the bedroom, which allows for that comfy King size bed back there, and two in this center aisle, one on either side, extending the dimensions of this inviting living room area. This *black* button opens and closes the bedroom area and a *yellow* button opens and closes the center slide-outs. Let me demonstrate."

Franklin's face offered clues that he was struggling to keep straight the green, blue, orange, black and yellow buttons with rapid eye movement, occasionally closing his eyes and silently mouthing the colors of the rainbow. But not slowed down, Mr. Withrow pushed the yellow button and the two living room slide-outs opened, sending the couch on one side and the dining room table on the other, out by several feet, enough to create a large living room area.

They all sat down in the newly expanded area as another aside came from Mr. Withrow. "Now, one caution, which I'm sure you are aware of, is that when these slide-outs close, there is considerable hydraulic pressure involved, so be sure that nothing is in the pathway of the rail for opening and closing each slide." He pointed to the space behind the co-pilot's seat, which marks the slide-out pathway.

"And another enhanced safety feature is a *secondary* emergency brake, right around the corner of this open area. Another push button, this one bright *red*, will set or release the emergency brake. This is in addition to the button at the driver's seat, just in case the driver is somehow incapacitated while at the wheel. In that event, a passenger can easily apply the brake, for everyone's safety."

Both Denise and Franklin – especially Franklin – were somewhat overwhelmed with all of this as they reviewed it all in their heads, with occasional fingers pointing to an imaginary tablet in the air, all trying to keep track of the full range of buttons: green, orange, blue, black, yellow, and now red.

"As you can see, our engineers have thought of everything, for your comfort *and* your safety. We want you to be happily using this RV for a long, long time!"

They smiled and nodded as they parted ways, Denise and Franklin to their car in the parking lot and Mr. Withrow to his office, where Ms. Carson, his boss, was waiting. She had been observing the entire encounter. "So they bought the sales pitch?" Mr. Withrow nodded and grinned very enthusiastically. "*And* the insurance policy?" she asked. "The *premium* policy!" he announced, gleefully. "The premium policy? But that one costs a fortune, and no RV owner has ever benefited from it, since most RVers are so conscientious about maintenance." But Mr. Withrow quickly added, "And they paid the 25 year premium, in full." "25 years! But…they'll be… nearly a hundred years old by then. Golly, did you pull a fast one! Congratulations!"

Chapter 4 – The *Long, Long Trailer* and a *Narrow, Narrow Bedroom*

The Great's retirement adventure began in the Spring of 2019 after the winter snows with its official launching at Yellowstone National Park. Franklin and Denise were sitting in the expanded living room, reviewing park brochures, and planning their schedule. Acting as the tour guide of the season, Franklin announced, "Oh, look, honey, there's a picture of the famous *Old Faithful Geyser*. We have to see that for sure. And there's a shuttle bus that can pick us up and take us right there." He opened up another brochure with the cover title of *How to Have a Safe RV Vacation* to see an article about bear encounters, which he read aloud. '*Bear attacks tourist! What you can do to protect yourself.*' He shuttered as he said, "Eeewh – I hope that doesn't interrupt our second honeymoon!"

"Oh, Franklin, put that aside. It's time for the *Family Movie Hour!* Since this is our second honeymoon, let's maintain an old tradition in our new home. Let's cuddle up and watch the movie!"

As they watched, Franklin had a hard time *not* thinking about that article, and he slipped into a day-dream about a bear encounter. It began with his being chased by a bear through the woods. He looked back to see that the bear was gaining on him, so he decided to change his running pattern to a zig-zag. Amazingly, the bear paused, looking puzzled, but then anticipated Franklin's next zag, and just as the bear was about to grab him, Franklin snapped out of his day-dream just in time to focus on the TV movie.

It was just in time to see the final scene of what they were watching, *The Long, Long Trailer*, in which Ricky and Lucy are hugging as the door of their trailer opens and closes in the rain. By coincidence, it was now raining outside their own RV, and Denise was the first to verbalize a thought they probably both shared. "That was such a wonderful movie, with such a romantic ending. Just like tonight. Don't you find the sound of rain on the roof of our new home so romantic?"

Franklin was practically purring. "Oh, yes, I do. I think it's time for bed, sweetheart…"

Hand in hand, they walked back to the bedroom, and they both tried their best to seductively undress, but partly because of their arthritis and partly because the bedroom was so small, they kept bumping into the walls. Franklin realized that the bedroom slide-out was closed, so he signaled to Denise his "aha" moment, and he majestically pushed the black button and the bedroom slide-out opened, giving them lots of room to crawl into their large bed.

An hour later after falling asleep, Franklin's earlier day-dream turned into a full scale nightmare, picking up where it had stopped. Now the bear grabbed Franklin and began to toss him back and forth from side to side. As Franklin dreamed this action, he tossed back and forth, from side to side, next to Denise. In one of his turning motions, he accidentally pushed the black button -- the bedroom slide-out button -- and the slide-out began to move in, making the bedroom smaller and smaller.

Denise and Franklin were both still half asleep as they began going through contortions trying to adjust to the closing wall and contracting bed. Finally, they woke up to the realization of the bedroom's shrinking dimensions. They continued their gymnastics, now reaching and stretching to try to save themselves by finding the black button. They each reached out several times to touch the elusive goal but could not actually press it as they were tossed by the continuously shrinking wall as the bed got smaller and their bodies tried to find stability on an uneven mattress.

Finally, before they were permanently sandwiched, Franklin was able to push the button. They looked at each other with a sigh of relief, pushed the button again to reopen the space, and began to remake their bed. They again settled in, but lay awake in a corpse-like silence.

Finally, Denise asked, "Franklin, is this what life in an RV is going to be like?" Franklin nodded his head in a 'yes' motion while responding, "Certainly not, my love. It'll be a wonderful, romantic, educational, life changing adventure!"

They both wore wide eyed looks of horror and spent the rest of the night fully awake, staring at the ceiling.

Chapter 5 – Flush!

The next day on a short hike from the RV, they shared a view -- from a distance -- of bison herds grazing in the field, and seeing an occasional fox, a family of deer, and birds from a variety of species circling above. Upon returning to the RV, they were relaxed but tired. After sitting on the couch in their new living room space, Denise was the first to speak. "Isn't it wonderful to be able to get out and hike on a beautiful, sunny spring day, at an amazing National Park? I'm so glad we came here." They hugged each other, and it was then that she was able to fully inhale the aroma of Franklin's heavy perspiration. "Oh, my, Franklin. You need a shower! And while you inaugurate the RV shower, I'll put the dishes in the dishwasher and start dinner."

Franklin proceeded to the shower and Denise to the kitchen. But before starting the dishwasher, she visited the toilet, which was in an enclosed area separated from the shower. The sound of the toilet flushing and that of Franklin's shriek were very nearly simultaneous. "Whoa! Honey! Next time you do that, will you just yell 'Flush!' so I can be prepared?"

"Oh, Franklin, I'm sorry. I agree that will be a new RV rule!" She returned to the dishwasher and was about to start it, but she thought for a moment and yelled out "Flush!" to warn Franklin of the change that will happen when the water rushed into the washer. "Thank you dear! That was very nice of you!"

Denise responded to her husband and to herself, "I guess we have a lot of new behavioral patterns to learn, being *real* RVers now…"

Chapter 6 – Free advice

Time marched on, as did their new adventure. It was now late Spring, 2019, on a cool mid-day drive into a new campground. They eventually found a secluded empty spot and each began their now-routine chores: Denise unpacking items from the upper cabinets, and Franklin setting up the RV. That included a number of tasks, one of which was pulling out the electrical cord from one of the storage bins under the RV and plugging it in to the lot's electrical pole.

As he continued the set-up tasks, a neighboring RV owner walked up to welcome him to the campground. "Hi there! Welcome to the prettiest campground in these here parts! I'm Walter."

"Hi, I'm Franklin."

"Traveling with your wife, and maybe grandchildren?"

"Oh, my wife is with me. Kind of a second honeymoon! As for the kids and grandchildren, well, they're so busy these days – and – well –"

"I understand. Sometimes that generation is just too busy to slow down enough to see the beauty around us." The two smiled then gazed at the landscape as they stood in an almost 'photo-op' pose facing a cloudless blue sky and the green mountainview surrounding them.

Walter broke the silence first with, "RV'ing is a special way to be close to nature, yet with all the comforts of home."

"Well, we're still adjusting to that. Hopefully we'll get there soon."

"So, Franklin, where did you come from and where are you headed?"

" *'Off into the sunset!'* Well, that was our goal when we started. You see, it all started with...oh, it's too long a story. We just came from Yellowstone, and I actually don't know where we're going from here. We just retired and since this is our 'retirement honeymoon' and our first trip in the RV, we're just going to … 'follow the wind!' and *'drive off into the sunset.'"* He had an embarrassed look for not being poetic enough to avoid repeating himself.

"Oh, I see. Well, the wife and I have been doing this for 21 years. It's a wonderful life!" As Franklin returned to his setting-up tasks, Walter saw that Franklin was having trouble keeping the electric cord plugged in, since he was stumbling over it while going back and forth behind the RV.

 "You know, Franklin, there are a lot of young kids in these campgrounds now-a-days, and they're so active, scurrying in between the RVs, they can sometimes trip over the electrical cord, so they've been known to accidentally unplug it. Oh, it's rare, but if I were you, I'd wrap that cord around the pedestal once, to be sure it stays in place, to keep those kids from disconnecting it."

"Oh, thank you. I'll do that." As Walter walked away, Franklin wrapped the electrical cord around the cement-based pedestal. Just then, he saw a group of children running around the campground, and he looked again at his electric cord. He decided to wrap it around twice – then after a beat – three times. As he walked away, he looked back and returned to add a *fourth* warp to be extra safe.

Chapter 7 – Earned wisdom

That night, as the honeymooners settled in to enjoy their old-fashioned oven-cooked dinner, Denise reflected, "You now, Franklin, I'm very impressed with our learning curve in adjusting to RV living – knowing where the buttons are for the slide-outs and the cabinets, learning the *Flush* warning, and your knowing all the right things to do to set up the RV. It all seemed so complicated at first, but you have learned all right the shortcuts."

Franklin welcomed the opportunity to congratulate himself. "Well, you are lucky to have married a genius, my dear! And I must admit that our fellow RVers are so welcoming and helpful. But, but I'm glad I'm genius enough to know good advice from bad advice!"

Chapter 8 -- The blackout

Very early the next morning – in fact at 4:00 AM – Denise and Franklin had already finished their breakfast. It was time for the drive-away checklist. Franklin took charge. "I'm glad I convinced you that we should leave before the sun is up, so we can get a good start. There's less traffic this early in the morning. And it's time you learned what's on the checklist for every time we pack up and leave. Let's go through it one more time." He began the list.

"Oven off and blue button pushed to keep the door closed?"
"Check."
"Pots and pans safely stored?"
"Check."
"Dining room table items cleared and folded?"
"Check."
"Green button pushed to close the over-head cabinets?"
"Check."
"Black button pushed to close the bedroom slide-out?"
"Check."
"Orange button pushed to close the bedroom door?"
"Check."
"Yellow button pushed to close the center slide-outs?"
"Check."

Denise now added one. "Sewage drain disconnected?"

Franklin confirmed, "Check. Ok then, we're ready for our next adventure!"

They settled into the driver's seat and co-pilot seat up front, and drove off, and as they did, only a camera from a drone above could have seen what was slowly unfolding.

It all started with a missed item on the check-list: unplugging the RVs electrical connection. Neither Franklin nor Denise could see that the electric cord was still plugged in. And they could not sense the drag on the RV as it stretched the cord while they slowly drove away from the lot. Nor could they see that the cord was wrapped so tightly around the pole that it finally pulled the cement base completely out of the ground.

For at least 2 miles, the RV dragged the cord, the cement base and at least 2 miles of underground electrical cables through the entire campsite. What they did notice was a slight sense of release when the cord snapped and the RV was free of its extra "passenger." But they could not see the sparks they left along their path, as they never looked in the rear view mirror, being so focused on "the road ahead" in their honeymoon adventure.

Only a drone camera could have seen, in a widening view, that the campground, still in a pre-dawn darkness, was entering a blackout, section by section.

Though they had no sense of the havoc behind them, what Franklin and Denise *could* see was a clear road ahead, as they dreamed of new adventures ahead.

And this was, in fact, just the beginning...

Chapter 9 – The road ahead

The drive to the next park was a long one. There were moments of fast-paced back-and-forth joking and laughing interspersed with periods of silence. One silence was interrupted as Denise started thinking out loud, an unusual move for an introvert. "You know, Franklin, I think it's time for us to invite some family and friends to visit us at a beautiful park to see us, the new RV and the campground. And to see how great RV living is."

"Do we have to invite Cousin Ralph?"

"No, no. We could make a list of who would be fun to have around, and who would appreciate the RV life-style." With that, Franklin was all-in. "OK, let's do it."

Denise was on a roll. "I'll send out a *Retirement News Letter* with an invitation." She began to make a list. "My sister, Janet, your cousins Bill and Claudia, your brother and his wife, their grandchildren, my old high school classmate, Cookie, and then Gary and Suzie and Michael and his wife, and Gloria and her husband, Randy, Chuck, and Shanta and Estephan, Maria and Kim, the two Dawns, and Jordan and Shatefa, and Sandra and Wilson, and Ralph and Sally…"

At this point, Franklin dived in, "Whoa – there's not enough room for all those people at the same time! And definitely **not** Ralph and Sally! And we'll need to split the list up and have two groups."

Denise agreed. "OK, that sounds like a good plan. I'll write the invitations and you plan the schedule." Then after two beats of silence, she added, "What about inviting Daniel and Myra? The grandkids would probably love to spend a vacation in an RV." Franklin was caught off guard. "Well, ah…" Trying to think of a good answer, "...they're…they're so busy, with their careers and getting the grandkids' own careers started. And Myra's husband is starting a new business. It's just not a good time for a visit." Knowing that there was more to the story, Denise pressed, "And...?"

"Well…you know what happened last Christmas, when we all got into that row over politics. I don't know what the world is coming to…or the country…and even for families. We're all so divided over politics these days. If they *did* visit, I don't know how we could start up a simple conversation without having a huge argument." Denise knew there was really more to it, and her look convinced Franklin to continue. "And, well, they don't look up to me like they did when they were kids. I kinda feel like I've let them down, and I don't know how I can guide them any more…"

Denise shifted to a more supportive press. "Well, maybe it's worth a try. Maybe they don't need guidance as much as, well, communication." "Maybe…" Just then, Franklin intentionally changed the subject by focusing on their trip. "Oh, I think our turn is coming up. Can you check the instructions we got from the park ranger?"

Eventually they made a turn and continued down a side road as they silently digested their conversation about Daniel and Myra.

Chapter 10 – A private text

Later that night, they settled into their new camp site. Denise was in their living room, with both the center slide-outs open, creating a very comfortable and casual space for working at the computer and preparing the invitations. "Franklin, I think there's room to add a couple of people to our list. We could invite your old college room-mate Ken and his wife. We haven't seen them since our 25th wedding anniversary party." Then, after a beat, "Franklin, do you think we are ready to send an invitation to Daniel and Myra?"

Ignoring her by pretending not to hear and being busy looking at brochures and maps for the activity schedule, Franklin observed, "We should plan the gathering when we are at one of the family-friendly parks. I'm calculating our route and options." He unfolded a large map and held it up, allowing him to hide his face from Denise, who, without Franklin watching, pulled up a text from Myra.

After exchanging texts, she said nothing, as would be expected from an introvert; but she did sigh.

Chapter 11 -- The guests arrive

Three weeks later, at a different campground the retired couple is learning that RV living was just the right mix of ongoing exploration of new parks and campgrounds blended with a repetition of relaxation, a recipe their marriage had been missing for some time. And they were looking forward to sharing that good news with their invited guests. Summer was approaching, as was the first gathering, which included children since school was out.

But there was a problem...

In response to their invitations, guests started showing up, *unannounced*, at the *same time*. Denise was sounding the alarm. "Franklin, I just got a text from 6 different people saying that their flights have arrived, and 5 people saying they should be here any minute and..." She was interrupted by a knock at the door.

Franklin answered with an extravert's welcome. "Gary, Suzie...welcome to...*paradise on wheels*!" Then, whispering an aside to Denise, "What happened? Didn't you split them up into two groups?"

The answer came sheepishly. "I guess I didn't make it very clear. And I forgot to ask them to make a reservation."

Without missing a beat, Franklin continued his greeting. "Welcome, welcome! Let me take your bag – err – bags." The guests had brought soft bags which he compressed as best he could, preparing to push them into the overhead cabinets. While he fidgeted with bags, Denise whispered back, "Well, they're here, so I guess we'll have to wing it."

Franklin pushed the green button to open the overhead cabinets (making a show of it to impress everyone) and they all began to stuff their suitcases and gift bags into small spaces like they were overstuffing the overhead cabinets on an airplane. The scene was quite frenetic, with arms and elbows swinging with luggage and everyone edging each other out like they were defending the home net in a basketball game.

About 30 minutes later, the battle of space versus people gave evidence as to who won – no one. After climbing over each other in the narrow center aisle, they finally collapsed onto every sofa and chair, spilling into the bedroom and bathroom and even sitting on kitchen counters, on the stove, in the front driver and co-pilot seats, with some sitting in laps, and children sitting on the floor – all in complete exhaustion.

Until Franklin broke the silence. "I have a great idea! Kids: how would you like to sleep in a tent tonight?" The responses came loudly and simultaneously, "Wow! That sounds great! Sure! Really?"

Then Jennifer and Chris, who had arrived with two teenagers, simultaneously interjected with heavy sarcasm, "And what about the *adults*, Franklin?" Making the best of it, "Oh, we have enough extra tents, sheets and blankets. We can *all* camp out. After all, some people call these RVs 'campers'! It'll be *fun*!"

Chapter 12 – A genius under the sky

Later that night, tourists who walked through the campground could see rows of tents alongside the Great's RV.

In the first were happy kids who were already asleep, dreaming about the best possible vacation: in a luxury RV and a rough camping tent – all in one trip.

In the next few were corpse-like adults, staring up through the netted top of the tent, wide awake. The rest of the adults were in the RV, with bodies everywhere, some asleep, some tossing and turning. They were on couches and chairs, on counter tops and one was even curled up in the shower.

In the last tent were Franklin and Denise, wide awake and silent. Until Franklin spoke up. "I don't want to make a big deal out of it, but having guests visit *was* your suggestion. So…any ideas?"

After an initial stressed look, Denise had an inspiration. "I know what we can do. There is more than one gift shop in the area, and there's a museum, and a park panorama, and the ranger stations, and hiking paths…let's organize a different tour for every day they're here."

To which Franklin responded, "I'm so glad I married a genius!"

They were now able to fall asleep under a star-lit sky.

Chapter 13 – A special gift is found

The next morning, one of the newly formed "tour groups" visited a gift shop at the park. Among them was one of the visiting couples, Katherine and Ted, looking at gifts.

Katherine could be heard by one of the shop employees, "You have to admit, they are trying." "Yes, *very* trying!" came a rapid follow-up from Ted. Katherine was equally quick with, "Oh, be serious, for a change. We need to buy them a gift." And Ted reluctantly agreed, "Well, OK, as long as it's a *cheap* gift."

The gift shop clerk who had been eavesdropping approached and suggested, "Oh, if you are looking for a very nice gift, which happens to be on sale this week, take a look at these framed art pieces. They feature park-specific scenery." Katherine and Ted were impressed, especially with the price tag. The clerk continued, "This is a collection of original water-colors by a regular visitor and park supporter. See, they are all signed and numbered."

"My, they *are* beautiful. Oh, here is one of a bear. I'm sure Franklin will like that one. Ted, I'll pay for this while you look in the hardware section for some hooks so we can hang it on the living room wall, as a surprise." Others in the group joined in buying souvenirs to be brought back to the RV, which added to the already over-packed and cluttered RV.

But this was just the beginning...

Chapter 14 -- A special gift is given

Back at the campground, a few hours later, a group of adults and children were playing croquet in a small playground near the RV. Katherine and Ted wanted their gift to be a surprise so they quickly and quietly sneaked their way into the RV and using a hammer and a nail, placed a hook on the living room wall and hung the painting of the bear. They waited patiently to see Franklin's expression when he came in after the croquet game.

Denise entered first with a group of players who stayed in the living room area while she and a few others went into the bedroom to store their gift shop purchases before preparing dinner. As Franklin entered the RV, he saw the bear painting ... and fainted!

Ted and Katherine looked at each other with surprise. Katherine spoke first. "I didn't know Franklin was **that** afraid of bears!"

Little did they know what had happened, and no one in the RV could actually see it. But Franklin sensed it.

Hidden inside the wall, a pneumatic hose had been pierced by the nail; the slow leak was virtually invisible, but nonetheless significant.

When Franklin regained consciousness, he could not speak clearly, but he tried to form the words of a warning – "Nail...pneumatic...bear... "

Ted tried to calm him. "Franklin, it's not a *real* bear, it's just a water..." But Franklin managed to interrupt. "You don't understand...it's..."

In his semi-conscious state, Franklin replayed in his head Mr. Withrow's warning about punctures to a pneumatic hose. "...if that nail has punctured a pneumatic hose..."

Just then, everyone in the RV heard a loud release of pressured air, and within seconds, the bedroom door automatically closed. As Mr. Withrow had explained, under this circumstance, it could only be opened by a repair specialist.

And that was, still, just the beginning...

Multiple voices could be heard from the bedroom, shouting "Open the door! Let us out of here! Help! Help!" Then the voice of Denise was distinguishable, "Franklin! How do we get out of here?"

Franklin's first response was, "I have no idea, dear. But let me think for a minute." He took a deep breath and tried to remember Mr. Withrow's tour of the RV, then he called out to Denise. "Go to the breaker box, on the back wall. Open it and look for a label – something about 'pneumatic system' and flip it."

Denise moved quickly to the breaker box, where she found these labels:

Lights
Kitchen appliances
Pneumatic system
Hydraulic system
Emergency shut-off

"I found it!"

After a beat, Franklin started breathing hard and fast and began shouting, "Flip the switch! Flip the switch! Quickly! Quickly!"

In her nervousness, Denise flipped the "hydraulic" switch by mistake, and the slide-outs immediately began to close, with a number of people in the shrinking area now entering a state of shock.

Trying to compose himself as the slide-outs started to close in, Franklin heard the ominous sound of the front RV door locking shut, the final signal of a full disaster to follow.
As the center of the RV began to fold inward, so did the exterior awning. Franklin could hear the sound of crinkling metal bars bending and snapping.

Though he could not see the outside damage in real time, he had a front row seat for viewing the interior chaos. The chairs and couches on both sides of the center aisle were moving the people who had been sitting in them, along with unfolded tables and scattered luggage. Everything was squeezing together – human and otherwise – in the path of the sliders.

Franklin finally diverted his attention from the chaos back to the solution, and shouted to Denise, "Find the *Emergency shut-off* switch, and flip it – quickly!"

At what appeared to be the very last minute, the slide-outs stopped moving, although they were already about 80% closed.

With all three slide-outs now closed and locked in that position, and the bedroom door also closed, and the front (and only) exit locked, Franklin finally realized the predicament – that none of the moving parts could be manually opened, and that the group was stuck in their tight and uncomfortable positions until a service specialist could arrive.

It was up to Franklin to explain that to the group.

And that was, still, just the beginning...

Chapter 15 – Later that night

Once the Emergency Rescue teams had arrived to assess the situation, several RV windows were forcibly cracked and removed as neighboring campers gathered to watch the circus-like acrobatics of old and young people manipulating their way through the small and oddly shaped window openings.

It was now the middle of the night, and everyone was safe. The guests were huddled in family groupings, as were their hosts. After some silent observation of the not-so-silent evacuations, Denise spoke up. "Did you call the RV people to have them send a repair specialist?" "Yes..." and after three beats of silence -- an unusual behavior for someone so extraverted, "...but they won't be able to be here for *three* days."

"*Three days!*" came the mixed tones of shock, anger and sarcasm. "So we're going to crawl in and out of these windows for – *three days!*"

Franklin thought for a second before speaking – a repeat of an unusual trait, since the circumstances required it. Then he looked up at the dawn-lit morning sky, and observed, in as much of an optimistic tone as possible, "At least the weather is nice."

Chapter 16 – Three hours later

Every RV within walking distance of the Great's RV could be seen with curious faces glued to, and looking out of their windows (from their interior comfort), watching the guests of Franklin and Denise gathered outside of the RV...

...in a hard pouring, steady rain.

Chapter 17 – The payout

Meanwhile, back at the ranch -- ah, the RV sales office -- Mr. Withrow was holding a receipt for the Great's RV repairs in one hand as the other was cradling his head.

Then slowly, he wrote out a check – the largest payout he had ever authorized, covering the full reimbursement for all expenses, per the insurance policy. His sigh did not bring any sense of relief.

But, still, it was only the beginning...

Chapter 18 – Later that week

Out of embarrassment, the RV was moved to a different location within the same park, but only after lengthy negotiations with the Park Administration, lawyers and accountants from both the park and the insurance company, and even FEMA (since it was in a National Park) and the county's equivalent emergency management agency.

And finally, the gathering of guests was able to move back into the RV, with a drawing each night for who would have to sleep in tents. For the most part, all appearances of the group's behavior returned to a state of quasi-normalcy. They were touring the park's diverse ecological niches, and of course, taking guided tours led by Park Rangers.

While on one tour, an experienced Park Ranger engaged the group with several mesmerizing tales from her years in the park. They were half real and half theatrical, all delivered by the would-be-actress-ranger, impersonating animals they might encounter in the park, with very entertaining improvisations as she encouraged the group's participation.

During these stories from Ranger Robin (she wore a prominent name tag with her name in large, red capital letters), Franklin was distracted by a circling bumble bee, which the Ranger used as inspiration for the description of prehistoric flying creatures attacking our human ancestors in that region of North America millions of years ago.

Then after a deep breath, composing herself for one of her "official" duties, she shared this announcement:

"Now, on a serious note, there have been some recent reports of *UBAs* – "unusual bear activity" in the park… "

Before she could continue, there were simultaneous expressions of conflicting responses:

Oh, my gosh!
What?
Really?
Where can we find them?
How tame are they here?
Can we pet the baby bears?
Are they real killers like the ones we see charging tourists on the internet?

With a wave of her hand, she continued. "…but you don't need to panic. Although an encounter with a bear *can* be deadly, you can live through the experience if you observe these four, cardinal rules:"

"1. Always carry a can of *Bear Spray*, which can be purchased in any one of our supply stores."
She withdrew her own can from a side holster, to show it to everyone.

"2. Avoid direct eye contact with the bear. Look down."

She motioned the 'eye to eye' contact with a 'two-fingers signal', pointing to her eyes, and then pointing downward.

"3. But raise your hands straight up!"

She theatrically demonstrated this, looking like she had just been held up by a gangster.

"And, 4 … *Slowly* back away."

And she did just that, intentionally backing into a *Beware of Bears* sign. She had staged this quite often, but the tour group responded with naïve amazement that such a 'coincidence' could have happened. This brought a mix of responses:

Oh, my gosh?
Can you believe that?
I never saw that sign before?
Was that a magic trick?
Amazing!

Then the entire group shared a relieving laughter, interrupted by Ranger Robin. "But seriously, whatever you do, **DO NOT RUN**. A bear is faster than you could ever imagine! And if you follow these rules, which you can use when you are in **TROUBLE**, you will probably live to tell the tale. Remember **TROUBLE** – *The Rules Of Unwinding a Bear's Live Encounter.*

She then concluded this part of the tour by saying, "And if the bear ever asks where you learned these rules...tell it 'I heard it from *Ranger Robin*!'"

She then gestured a final theatrical-style curtain-call bow before the group, which brought a round of applause. The members of the group were now nodding and mimicking bear movements and role playing Ranger Robin's TROUBLE guidelines.

Denise looked around for Franklin, only to discover that Franklin was still dodging the bumble bee. "Did you hear those rules, Franklin?" Caught off guard, he quickly mumbled, "Oh, yeah. Every word," as he ducked both the circling bee and the question.

Ranger Robin had one last duty. "Before we finish, I am obligated as an official Park Ranger..." as she pointed to her Ranger Badge, "...to warn you that a rabid squirrel has been sighted in the park. It is a very rare, endangered species of the squirrel family, found *only* in this park area, so if you see a strangely acting squirrel, avoid it, call a Ranger, but **DO NOT HARM IT!**"

Denise pulled Franklin aside, finally trying to get his attention away from the bee, "Franklin, did you hear that?" Franklin dutifully nodded, even though it was obvious he was only listening to the buzz around his head. "I think you should buy a can of that bear spray, for *any* crazy animal out there. You go to the supply store and I'll take the group to the tourist center."

And off they went in different directions.

But this, still, was just the beginning...

Chapter 19 – The stealthy stalking

As Franklin walked up to the entrance of the Supply Store, he was unaware of the squirrel that had followed him.

Upon entering, Franklin was greeted by an older store clerk. "Good morning. How can I help you?" Franklin answered, "I'm looking for a can of *bear spray*." "Ah, yes, that's a very popular item at this time of the year. We have several right here on our display counter." After handing him a can, he added, in a serious and slow tone, "Now, I am obligated to inform you that, while life-saving, this spray is very potent. When pointed toward a bear, it can temporarily blur an animal's vision and cause significant disorientation. But that could also happen to a *human*, if the spray is accidentally misdirected. So, use it carefully!"

"I understand. Thank you." And with that, Franklin paid the clerk and exited the store, unaware that the same squirrel who had followed him to the store was apparently now stalking him.

It picked up Franklin's scent and followed him at a safe distance, so as not to be discovered. Franklin walked at a brisk pace, but paused once, sensing someone – or some *thing* -- was following, and the savvy squirrel quickly hid behind a tree.

Relying on his sixth sense which told him he was not alone, Franklin shared a puzzled look with nearby hikers, and then turned in a full circle to look around the area. Not seeing the squirrel, he continued his walk to the RV.

And the squirrel continued its stealthy, determined stalk.

And this was, indeed, just the beginning...

Chapter 20 – The intrusion

Upon arriving at the RV, Franklin opened the door with one hand while carrying the bear spray in the other. He paused for a moment (he could later not remember why), allowing just enough time for the squirrel to enter first, between his feet.

Franklin wasn't sure what it was that brushed by his feet, but it surprised him enough to reach out to the co-pilot's chair for stability and that caused him to drop the bear spray. He didn't realize it at the time, but it landed behind the co-pilot chair, next to the slide-out opening space, in the critical pathway for the center slide-outs.

He began a frantic search for the squirrel, up and down the center aisle but he could not find it, so he decided to check the overhead cabinets to see if it *somehow* got into one of them. So he pushed the green button to open them, and by accident, in his surprised and worried state, he also pushed the blue oven door button as well.

When the overhead cabinet doors opened, all the compressed bags, gift shop items and other miscellanea stored there, popped out and flew everywhere. That startled the squirrel, who had hidden under a couch, so it ran for cover, finding safety in the open oven.

Franklin didn't see this motion, and unaware of its now hiding in the oven, he assumed the squirrel had escaped out the RV door, which was still open. So he closed the oven door and the RV door and began to collect all the overhead items.

The squirrel was now trapped -- in the oven.

And this, still, was only the beginning...

Franklin managed to get everything back into the overhead cabinets just as the group of visitors returned from a hike after the tour, and, playing thoughtful hosts, Franklin and Denise encouraged everyone to relax as they began to prepare dinner. Denise began to pull items out of the refrigerator and Franklin set the oven to preheat to 425 degrees.

Before long, the odor of roasted squirrel was smoking up the RV with more than an aroma – with a stifling stench.

But that, still, was just the beginning...

Chapter 21 – The aftermath

It didn't take long for a crowd to gather – a very large crowd.

There were park rangers, the fire department, the rescue squad, members of the press with news camera people, and, of course, RV neighbors who were most disturbed by the ever-spreading smell which would take days to air out of any RV in that section of the park.

A senior Park Ranger approached Franklin with a stern expression. "You do realize...that innocent little squirrel was an endangered species -- right?" The Ranger took out a citation booklet and began to write out a ticket. "That's going to result in a hefty fine, for cruelty and…" as tears began to appear, "possibly ending that poor creature's lineage...for all time." Then regaining composure, "The address for your payment is on the back of the citation."

The Ranger started to walk away but turned to add, "Oh, and since that squirrel may have been rabid, you…and your guests…will need to remain here at the campground, quarantined, for a week, to be sure that no one has rabies." And adding with a slight sarcasm, "and to allow enough time to clear the odor of cooked squirrel before anyone else camps in this spot."

It was still cold weather each night at this time of year at this location, but for a week, the Greats and all of their guests had to stay inside the RV with all the windows open to clear the air. They sat, huddled in layers of winter jackets, shivering and casting scowls at Franklin, wishing they had never visited.

But this, still, was only the beginning...

To make matters worse, the story hit the news feeds and headlines appeared nationwide:

"*Camper Cooks Cute Chippy*" and
"*Squirrel Species Smoked*"

with sub-headings of

"*Innocent and Endangered Squirrel Found Locked and Roasted in RV Oven*"

This resulted in the presence of demonstrators pacing outside the RV, around the clock, with signs reading --

"SOS" for "Save Our Squirrels"

It was yet another humiliating entry in the diary of retirement.

Chapter 22 – The release of the captives

A full week later, the guests were packed and eager to leave, as Franklin and Denise waved to each one as they left the RV, all in silence, with nothing but glares.

Finally, Franklin and Denise were allowed to move to another park.

But this, still, was only the beginning...

As they drove away, the now-forgotten can of bear spray was resting in the dangerous pathway of the slide-outs...not yet crushed...but awaiting the opportunity.

Chapter 23 – A new group of visitors

Three weeks later, another group of visitors joined the Greats for a hopefully calmer getaway at a new park, but at the same time the bags were again stuffed in the overhead cabinets and the center aisle was always overcrowded as bodies constantly bumped into each other,

Franklin motioned for Denise to meet outside the RV, where he whispered to her, "What now, Ms. Genius?"

"I think a visit to the camp's new Community Center, with the Olympic size pool would work," came her suggestion.

Which is what happened.

But this was just the beginning...

As they arrived, Denise realized she had forgotten their registration ticket, required for entry. "Franklin, I'll stay with the group if you go back to the RV to get it. It's on the dining room table." Franklin dutifully responded, "OK. I'll be right back," as he headed down the main walkway toward the RV.

Until...he noticed a short-cut trail through the wooded area behind the RV lots.

It didn't take long for the inevitable to happen: a bear encounter!

Franklin's first response was to reach for his bear spray holster...which was empty. A violation of Ranger Robin's Rule #1. That led to his second response...the look and feel of panic.

Franklin then stared directly into the bear's eyes, a violation of Ranger Robin's Rule #2, which evoked a predictable response from the bear.

As the bear showed signs of an oncoming charge, Franklin began waving his hands like a bird thinking he could "wave off" an attack, a violation of Ranger robin's Rule #3.

Franklin had only an instant to make his next decision, as he thought out loud to himself and the bear, in typical extravert fashion, "Time to run!" The *last* violation of Ranger Robin's *last* Rule.

As Franklin began to run, he unconsciously recalled the similar scenario from his earlier dream, and his autonomic nervous system kicked in and led Franklin on a zig-zag football pattern, back and forth.

Unlike the dream-encounter, this time the bear is temporarily *confused* by Franklin's change of running pattern, since the bear was unfamiliar with the game of football. And quite remarkably, Franklin made it to safety in the RV, with the bear only inches behind him.

Franklin was so mentally rattled and his legs so wobbly, now that his parasympathetic nervous system was kicking in after the stress response, that he reached out for stability, causing his left foot to hit the hidden can of bear spray, resting behind the co-pilot's seat, where it had fallen earlier.

And this was, obviously, just the beginning...

His misstep led to a full trip, and on the way down, with his arms flailing about for something to grab onto, he managed to hit the yellow button which started to close the slide-outs.

As the slide-outs moved in, Franklin was suddenly conscious enough of the bear spray can and its location -- in the direct path of the high-powered hydraulic closing slide-out, which could easily crush the can, causing an explosion of the powerful bear spray.
His semi-conscious brain simultaneously merged internal recordings of warnings from Mr. Withrow and the Supply Store Clerk.

Realizing time was short, he heroically dodged toward the can to move it toward safety. But it was too late, and his face was now within inches of the exploding spray.

The sting of the spray blurred both his vision and his mental orientation. In his confusion, he leaned against the green button which opened all the storage cabinets, and again, everything popped out and littered the entire center area. That motion startled him enough to focus on pushing the green button again, to close the cabinets, but by a combination of a mistake and a remaining disorientation, he managed to push the red button which released the emergency brake...

Which caused the RV to begin its roll down a slight grade. (In all the commotion of preparing for more guests, Franklin had postponed a full check-list of stabilizing the RV's position, including safety blocks to prevent what was about to happen.)

And this was, no doubt, just the beginning...

The RV was rolling toward the Community Center in direct aim of the swimming pool, where Denise and their guests were innocently splashing and laughing away their final moments before the impending impact. But once they realized that they were in the path of the RVs journey, they all began to scramble, with some zig-zag movement of their own, reflecting indecision about what was the best path to safety.

The RV gained speed as it continued downhill, not even slowing as it broke though the pool's fence. The only thing that slowed it down was its plunge into the pool.

Amidst the screams, Franklin was now conscious enough to hear glass shattering, metal bending -- and the last sound he remembered -- an exploding tire. It was the only sound that brought a smile to his agonized face, recalling that he was wise enough to purchase the premium insurance package, which covered even the tires!

Chapter 24 – Mr. Withrow's demise

A month later, Mr. Withrow was sitting at his desk. His supervisor, Ms. Carson, was holding – or perhaps gripping -- a large stack of bills and receipts. "We paid out *how **much*** to the Greats for this insurance policy?" she asked.

Mr. Withrow shook his head back and forth, afraid to answer, and also afraid to hear what came next:

"You're fired!"

Chapter 25 – Retirement, phase 2

It took several months for all the paperwork, including legal and other settlements to a long list of people and places, to be finally cleared up. But the premium insurance policy actually paid off. Enough for Franklin and Denise to move into *Stone River Village*, an upscale over-55 retirement community in a warm region of the country, where it was still summer-like during the Fall of 2019.

It all began in a *new* sales office...

Franklin and Denise were having coffee in the Model Homes section of the Sales Offices, hosted by Ms. Washington, a senior sales agent. "I'm so glad you have decided to move into our fun and fantastic community. In a minute, we'll go on a tour of our model homes, but, first, let's see, if you have an idea of the square footage you would like." And then after a brief pause, "Of course…" almost singing as if it were a running sales joke, "… the bigger the floor plan, the bigger the price!"

Franklin responded first. "Well, we just received an insurance settlement from our recent RV -- ah -- accident. Would this get us into an entry level model?" He handed the check to MS. Washington, whose face could not hide her gleeful surprise.

"Well, now, Mr. Great – *this* will get you into our largest – and best – model! Yes, indeed! If you just sign here, we'll look at that floor plan."

Without hesitation, Franklin signed the contract.

"On our way to the model, you can take a look at our property brochure. We have a Recreation Center with an Olympic size pool, an on-site café, a large picnic and playground area, and an award-winning golf course."

Denise lit up and spoke quickly, an unusual introvert behavior. But the word "golf" had triggered something. "Oh, Franklin, a golf course!" Then to Ms. Washington, "You know, I was the captain of my college golf team."

At that point, Franklin interjected condescendingly, "Oh, now, that was a long time ago, sweetheart. I'm sure the competition *here* will be pretty tough." But Denise took that as a challenge. "Oh, I'm still pretty tough enough!" She grabbed the brochure from Ms. Washington's hand and led them all out of the office.

Chapter 26 – The challenge

About a month later, after moving into their wheel-less home, Franklin and Denise were washing the dinner dishes in their new open-floor-plan kitchen family room. "Oh, Franklin, this home is just perfect for us. Everything is sparkling new, and practical and beautiful! And the neighborhood is so … welcoming and … pristinely kept. You know, Franklin, I think we should get to know our neighbors right away, as we settle in. After all, I doubt if this residence will ever roll down a hill!" Then with a romantic smile, "Looks like this will be our final home."

"Which I hope it will be for a long, long time," added Franklin, before a kiss.

"I think you're right," he added. "And it will be important to start making a good impression. Like the saying goes, 'You only have one chance at a first impression.'"

"Right. And I'd like *my* first impression to be more than that of a 'homebody housewife'. I was thinking about making an impression on the *golf course*. After all, I did win three trophies during my golf career in college."

Franklin's tone now changed. "Denise, you have my blessing to give that a try. And I'll work as ..."

having to pause to come up with something,
"a...a...good landscaper. After all, the time for
mowing the lawn is coming up soon!"

"Great, Franklin. I'll go to the pro shop in the
morning." And after a hug, they finished the dishes.

Chapter 27 – The pro shop

Early the next day, Denise found her way to the golf course, and to the entrance of the *Stone River Village Golf Shop.*

"Good morning. I'm Denise Great. We just moved in and I'd like to know about your golf course." The Village's Golf Pro was Ms. Stacy Garrison, a golfer with an impressive resume, as indicated by the multiple plaques on the shop's wall, which Denise noticed right away. "Looks like you had quite a career!"

"Oh that's just a sampling. You should see my trophy wall at home! But you're not here to assess my career; you're here to help *yours,* right?"

"Oh, I'm not a professional. Just a decent amateur looking for a challenge."

"Well, welcome to *Stone River* – home of the best and *most challenging* golf course in the state. Are you a long-time golfer?"

"Well, I played in college. I was the team captain. But, it *has* been a while."

"Oh, golfing is like riding a bike. *Once you get the knack, you'll always get it back!* And your timing is excellent. Would you like to sign up for the *Stone River Classic,* coming up soon?"

"Oh, I don't know if I..."

"Oh, don't let the name scare you. It's an annual local competition, just among our residents. And there will be trophies – for the longest drive, and for anyone who gets a hole-in-one."

"Well..."

"You've got nothing to lose..."

Half to herself, half to Ms. Garrison, Denise rallied her most extraverted skills and confidently spoke her thoughts aloud, "...and everything to prove. I'll do it!"

"Great! Let's fill out the forms, so you will qualify for any trophies." Ms. Garrison placed a form on the counter and Denise began to fill it in. "I assume you have your own clubs?"

Denise didn't want to appear to be a complete amateur, with no clubs. "Ah...no," then quickly thought of a cover. "We haven't gotten everything from the movers, yet."

"That's no problem. You can rent them. Then you will probably need a box of golf balls, too." As Ms.

Garrison placed a box on the counter, Denise looked at the price tag. "Gosh, these are pricey!"

"They are, but they are also guaranteed for life, and each ball has a registered number stamped on it, so if you ever lose a ball in the rough or even off the course, we will find them. We hire some local teenagers to search the grounds every weekend to find lost balls, and, since they *are* registered, we will return them to you, free of charge. So the price is worth it. You will never have to buy another golf ball again! That's our guarantee."

Denise thought for only a second, and assertively responded, "Let's do it!"

"Great. When you complete the forms and I'll give you a tour of the shop and the adjacent Common Room. Perhaps some of the other golfers will be there this morning."

Sure enough, as they began the tour. Ms. Garrison spotted three women who always sign up for the event. "Ladies, let me introduce you to our newest member, and our latest registrant for the *Stone River Classic.* Joan, Betty and Mary, meet Denise." They exchanged greetings as Ms. Garrison continued her introductions. "Joan is a *four-time* winner of the *Classic.* She's probably the best golfer in the Village – even counting the men!"

Joan demurely offers, "Oh, I'm not the best, I'm sure," but then giving Denise a direct and clearly threatening stare, "But I *am* sure that I am *pretty good* -- better than anyone one else since we moved here!"

Mary quickly and subordinately added, "*Pretty good*? She is a *terror* on the green." Pause. "Not that we are trying to *intimidate* you…"

Denise decided to stand her ground. After all, 'you only have one chance at a first impression.' "Oh, of course not. And even if you were, since I was the *captain* of my college golf team, I can handle the intimidation."

"*College* team?" offered Joan with a smirk and a condescending tone.

Betty tried to lower the tension. "I'm sure you can, sweetie. It's all just a friendly little *family competition.*" But Denise was up for the engagement. "Well, thank you for the very friendly welcome to the family." Betty tried again to decelerate things. "We're just here to wish you luck, honey."

As they started to part ways and leave the Common Room, Mary added, "Oh, by the way, Joan is the only golfer here who has won *two* trophies in *one* game. No one has ever matched that." Pause. "Just so you have a goal…"

The three women giggled as they left the room.

But Denise now had a goal – and this was only the beginning...

Chapter 28 – The dream

Later that evening, as Denise and Franklin were washing the dinner dishes, Franklin spoke up about the tournament. "I'm very proud of you, Denise. After all these years, taking on such a challenge."

"Oh, I just hope I won't embarrass you – or myself. Especially after that 'warm welcoming committee.'"

"Don't worry about them. You'll do fine. It's just that it's your first tournament in years – and your first one *here*. It's normal to be a little nervous. Just remember what the golf pro told you – 'You have nothing to lose.'"

"But I worry if I am worthy of being a member of our new community." To which Franklin responded, with a hug, "Sweetheart, you are *very* worthy of being a member of our family, and that's what really matters."

Chapter 29 – The tournament

The *Stone River Classic* began on a clear, bright and warm day, with a crowd of locals ready to 'ooh' and 'awe' at each swing. At the first tee, Betty and Mary went first, then Joan stepped up to a welcoming reception and a loud applause, which she acknowledged with a bow. Her swing resulted in a very long drive, with the ball reaching the green -- almost an ace, a hole-in-one.

Joan paused before walking on, to take a slow look at Denise, with a challenging "beat that" look. Denise then quietly approached the tee box, took a few practice strokes, and then stepped up, clearly hesitant, for a real swing. It resulted in a terribly amateur shot which sliced into the rough. She looked down, as though the venture was already lost even before they arrived on the first green.

The 5th hole had a lengthy stretch of fairway, and Joan, Mary, Betty had all unsuccessfully tried to reach the green with one swing from the tee. When Denise stepped up, she took a deep breath before a graceful but strong swing, and the ball flew high into the air, struck a bird, and then bounced *off* the bird and *into* the hole for the first hole-in-one of the match. Joan, Mary and Betty all froze in shocked horror.

Then Joan regained her focus and shouted to the judge, "That has to be a foul!" "Yes, ma'am. It w*as* a fowl – the bird was actually an endangered species." "Not *that* kind of fowl…I mean a *golf* foul. Surely, it has to be disqualified as a hole-in-one."

After a long minute of reviewing the rule book for the tournament, the judge answered, "The rules do not say anything about a 'bird ricochet drive'. Therefore, the hole-in-one qualifies for a trophy."

Joan revived her angry stare toward Denise. But Denise was now prepared to stiffen up and stare back.

But this, still, was only the beginning...

At the 11th hole, Joan, Mary and Betty all got their golf balls on the green with their first drives, but again, missed the golden goal of a hole-in-one. Their caddies were already on the putting green, estimating the distances from the flag, carefully watching over the first three balls.

Denise stepped up for her shot from the tee, and with her own long drive the ball flew high, pausing at the arc's peak, then picked up speed as it headed toward the green – and toward Joan's caddy, who was looking at Joan and not at the ball in the air.

The ball struck the caddy in the forehead, knocking her out, but bouncing off her head and into the cup – for another hole-in-one!

Joan now aimed a stare at the judge. "Please tell me there is a rule disqualifying *human* assistance in the flight of a ball?" But after reviewing the rule book again, the judge responded, "There are no rules mentioning a 'human ricochet drive'. The hole-in-on stands. Another trophy!"

Amazingly, this, still, was only the beginning...

Finally reaching the 18th and final tee, the angry but determined trio -- Joan, Mary and Betty – all hit long drives. Denise stepped up to the tee, and with her own strong drive, the ball flew high into the air -- and out of sight.

But in the living room of a home on the edge of the golf course sat an elderly couple, having their mid-day tea. The sound of shattered glass startled them. "What just happened?" "It's a golf ball! Someone just hit a golf ball through our window!" "I told you we should never have bought the model house closest to the golf course."

One of them picked up the ball and noticed the markings. "Look! This is one of those registered golf balls. We can trace the owner and get reimbursed for all this damage!"

Chapter 30 – The trophies

Later that afternoon, the players and fans of the *Stone River Classic* had gathered in the *Recreation Center Common Room* for the Awards Ceremony. Joan, Mary, Betty and Denise were at the host table under the banner reading, "*The Annual Stone River Classic Tournament.*"

As the emcee, Ms. Garrison tapped a wine glass at the table to get everyone's attention. "First place by the numbers, the winner of this year's competition – we all know her – *Joan!*" to which there was an obedient applause. With enthusiasm, she continued, "And the score leaders then, by rank, Betty, Mary...." and her enthusiasm whittled down to a demeaning reference, "and in *last* place, our newest member, Denise."

But her tone shifted with the next set of awards. "And now, our special *Stone River Classic* trophies. First, we have a trophy for a hole-in-one on the 5th hole. A first time for that hole. It goes to...*Denise Great!* Here is your trophy..." Then in an almost whisper, "along with a fine for killing an endangered species bird."

"And next, we have a trophy for *another* hole-in-one at the 11th hole. It goes to... *Denise Great!* Here is your trophy..." Then again in an almost whisper, "along with the medical bill for the injured caddy."

"And finally, a trophy for the longest shot on record, at the 18th hole – long enough to enter a home outside the golf course! It goes to ...yes... *Denise Great!* Here is your trophy…" Then, once more, in an almost whisper, "along with a bill for repairing their window."

"This is now the *new course record* for the number of trophies in one match -- *three*. Denise, your name will appear on a plaque here at the *Stone River Village Community Center Golf Club*. Congratulations."

As Ms. Garrison uncovered the already hanging plaque, Joan did not bother to stare; she simply walked away.

Chapter 31 – The trophies find their way home

That night, Denise and Franklin were standing by the mantle where the new trophies now lived, on full display for anyone who entered the house. "I'm so proud of you! Would you look at the shine on those trophies!" They couldn't resist taking dozens of cell-phone pictures of Denise pointing to or holding each trophy, which would quickly appear on social media.

"Oh, I was just lucky, that's all." Franklin quickly responded, "Lucky? Three times? No way! You were spectacular!" Then under his breath and after a beat, "I only wish I had just *one* trophy for the 38 years with W*ilson, Wilson, and Wilson*." Then, surprisingly, Franklin added, "You know, Daniel and Myra would be *really* proud of you. Did you call them?"

"I did…and…"

But *not* surprisingly, Franklin quickly changed the subject. "You know, I've thought about taking up golf myself, now that I am married to a *pro* who could give me free lessons."

"Franklin, I think…"

Sensing that he needed to avoid what was to follow. "Well *I* think you are very, very special. And the next time we walk into the Recreation Center, I'll be the proudest husband in *Stone River Village*."

Resolving herself to a later conversation about Daniel and Myra, Denise simply hugged Franklin and wished for a later opportunity to talk.

Chapter 32 – The HOA Welcome Kit

A week later, the happy couple was settling in, finding new routines and a new place to display the trophies -- on a shelf where old dishes were usually displayed. It all began to feel like home, and a much calmer one than the RV. One of their shared morning routines was to sit around the large dining room table to read the local newspaper, a fading but valued tradition, and open the daily mail.

Franklin noticed an oversized envelope from the *Stone River Villages*. "Oh, here it is!"

"Here is what, Franklin?"

"The *HOA Welcome Kit*".

"HOA? Remind me…"

"The Home Owner's Association"

"Does it have information about the Recreation Center hours? And if we can host parties there? So our future guests can see the special golf plaque?"

"Well, I'm just opening it – I don't know." He continued to unseal the envelope as Denise continued her train of thought. "I'd love to invite some neighbors to a card party."

"Oh, here are the HOA rules. Let's see…" He unfolded a brochure listing the community rules, and began reading aloud..."

"We, at the *Stone River Village Community*, consider the safety and the appearance of our neighborhood as top priorities, for good living, and good property values."

Franklin and Denise smiled at each other, in agreement. "We made such a good choice to finally settle here," Denise offered with a sigh.

Franklin continued reading. "Consequently, our members have voted on the following 3Rs -- *Rules for Right Residing*. All rules must be observed, under penalty of a fine."

1 -- Any landscaped trees must be approved for size, type and shape, and trimmed to under 8 feet in height. These trees were selected as appropriate for warm climates. (He mumbles through a list of tree types before getting to the next rule.)

2 -- Any lawn sprinkler systems must not turn on after 6AM or before 6PM.

3 -- Garage doors cannot be left open when unattended.

4 -- Lawn tools cannot be left in the yard, unattended.

5 -- The enclosed color cards in Set 1 are the only approved house exterior colors.

6 --The enclosed color cards in Set 2 are the only approved house interior colors.

7 -- The lawn must be maintained to assure the following healthy growth -- specifically...

a. The grass cannot be taller than between 1.875" and 2.125". Enclosed are measuring stakes to assure proper grass height. (Franklin pulled out two small baggies of tooth-pick sized measuring sticks.)

b. The grass must fall within a designated range of green color; see the color cards in Set 3.

c. Any grass that has a yellowish appearance indicates that the home owner has not properly maintained the lawn.

8 – Any violations, including multiple or overlapping instances, may result in an increased fine.

Franklin had all three sets of color-coded cards, the tooth-pick stakes, and the rules spread out before him on the table. Looking discouraged and wondering if the move from the old RV days of freedom was a mistake, his expression changed when he saw something else in the envelope. "Oh, and look at this!"

He held up a large coupon card. "In order to maintain the 3Rs and the safety and appearance of our beautiful community, a $100 coupon toward the annual HOA fee will be awarded to any member who reports each and every HOA violation." With a grin – and a plan -- Franklin quietly put the coupon card, the color cards, and the baggies of measuring sticks, into his pocket, without saying a word – a challenge for a happy extravert.

Denise was on another page. "Franklin, I'm so glad we moved into a *regular* house, with such high expectations for keeping up good appearances, and in a wonderful community. This feels like a *real* retirement." To which Franklin responded, "It's a good thing I bought that premium insurance policy. Without that payout, we would never have been able to afford such a nice, roomy and private home."

It was then that they both noticed that their home was not so private. A couple of small lizards (common in this geographic area) were crawling onto the back porch and threatening to enter the living room by way of an open sliding door.

Denise calmly observed, "Yes, roomy but not so private!" And franklin added, "Oh, one of our neighbors is a retired zoologist. He says those critters are indigenous to the area and very prolific *only* here. They have just been placed on the *endangered species* list." He picked one up to remove it and Denise hastily warned him, "Oh, Franklin, be careful! Don't hurt it. We don't want any protestors here, in **this** neighborhood. It won't add to our 'first impression.' Remember the squirrel?"

Franklin briefly imagined a demonstration in the front yard, with a group of protesters carrying signs reading, "SOL – Save Our Lizards!", and he quickly agreed. "Oh, right," and very gently walked the lizard to the outside to release it.

And while outside, he noticed the condition of the grass. "Speaking of lawn care, I think it's time to mow!" And Denise took advantage of the opportune open door for, "You know, if Daniel or Myra were here, they could help with chores like that…" Franklin nodded but otherwise ignored the comment, and went into the garage to get the lawn mower.

And while mowing the lawn, he stopped for a moment to notice the lawn of the neighbor to the *right* side of his house. He paused to think about it, and pulled the coupon and color cards and the measuring sticks from his pocket. He looked around to see if anyone was watching him, and thinking no one was, he stealthily examined the color and the height of the grass, then pulled out a pencil and a piece of scrap paper to make notes. He also thought to take a several photos with his cell phone to document his new-found evidence.

Unseen by Franklin, there was someone in a neighbor's window, viewing the events with a critical scowl. But Franklin was on a roll, as he stealthily moved to the neighbor's lawn to the *left* side of his house, repeating the same measurements, while yet another neighbor watched with an expression of disapproval.

But Franklin's face showed anything but disapproval; there was a distinct grin.

And this, still, was just the beginning...

Chapter 33 – A reward and a plan

For days, Franklin was sure to be the first to collect the daily mail. Then...it arrived. A receipt from the HOA, acknowledging a $400 discount on his next bill. Whispering to himself, "Nice – coupon money for Christmas," Denise asked, "What was that, Franklin?" "Oh, nothing, dear."

"You know, not only is the house so roomy and large, we have such smart – and nice – neighbors, don't we, Franklin?" A blush of guilt was hard to hide, already wondering if his HOA plan would backfire, so Franklin thought of something nice to say about a nearby neighbor. "Speaking of nice neighbors, guess who's living right across the street? Do you remember when you were a child, listening to a radio and TV comedy called *The Aldrich Family*?"

"Oh, my. Yes I do. But why bring that up?"

"And the little boy who played their son, Henry?"

"Yes. His mother kept calling him --- 'Hen-reeeeeeeee! Kind of like me calling "Dan---eeeeeeeee!"

Franklin didn't bite on the reference to their son; now was not a time for that conversation. He returned his focus to the neighbor across the street.

"Yes, that's the show! Well, that actor is one of our neighbors – Robert Casey! I met him yesterday as I was looking at his lawn – ah, I mean *crossing* his lawn to get to the mailbox. He's getting up in years, but I recognized him right away. Oh, and he appears to be very shy, so please don't mention this to anyone; he moved here when he retired, incognito, to escape autograph seekers. I'm sure he doesn't want to be bothered by a bunch of older groupies!"

"Oh, I won't say a word. But it's interesting to know that he came *here*. Oh, Franklin, this is such an idyllic and diverse community. A famous actor across the street, an IT person a few houses away, retired teachers, doctors and scientists. We are so fortunate. We should find ways to be *extra* kind to all of our neighbors. "

Franklin started to choke on his morning coffee, but Denise went on. "I think we should host a family gathering – and Christmas is coming up and that would be a wonderful time to let everyone know how good things turned out here after the..." pausing, not sure how to best phrase what she was thinking. "You know, the relatives are still a bit worried about us after the 'RV event.'"

Relieved to shift the topic from the neighbors, Franklin agreed. And Denise saw the open door. "And it would be a special time to invite Daniel and

Myra." And it worked. Franklin was willing to say anything to keep the conversation from trending toward the specific neighbors to the left and right.

Denise jumped up and announced, "I'll prepare the invitations; you plan the schedule."

And this, too, was just another beginning...

Chapter 34 – A revised plan

A couple of weeks before Christmas, their morning routine was continuing to settle in. And one of those routines was a morning 'check-in' to review that day's 'to-do list.'

Denise was first. "Whew. The invitations have all been sent out -- to 18 relatives and friends. And I have a map all worked out identifying where everyone can stay. There are enough bedrooms for the couples, with a spill-over room upstairs for all the children to sleep on the floor. It will be like 'camping out' – only with no closing walls or rain! We could even set up a tent in that room, if the children wanted it! But if we have to, the little ones could sleep on the sofas here, in the living room."

Franklin chimed in, on cue. "And I have a daily schedule all worked out." As Franklin was sharing his schedule plans, Denise was reading through day's the mail.

8:00 AM -- A brisk walk to the Recreation Center; the exercise will be good for all ages.

9:00 AM – The pool opens and everyone can take a swim or sunbathe. The net will be set up in the far end of the pool for water volleyball, and there's a section roped off for laps, for the serious swimmers.

Noon----- lunch in the *River Munch Café,* so we
don't have to prepare every meal *here*!

Denise interrupted, with a grin, even as she kept
opening the mail, "Good thinking; it can be chaos if
there are too many cooks in the kitchen!" But once
she opened one letter, her grin faded away."

"Franklin ----"

Ignoring Denise and continuing his schedule...

1:00 PM – board games in the Recreation Center for
the younger set, and the daily Yoga class for the
seniors in the gym area. Or, watching the big
screen TV in the common area.

"Franklin ----"

Continuing the plan for each day,

3-5 PM – nap time for the little ones -- and the older
ones – while a few, select "cooks" help in the
kitchen, preparing dinner.

5-8 PM – dinner, desert, conversation, and
unwinding.

With increasing volume and concern, "*Franklin*!"

8-10 – *Family Movie Hour*.

10 PM – lights out!

"*Franklin*, this just came in the mail…" She handed him the letter – from the HOA, which Franklin read out loud.

"Dear residents. We are informing you of our plans for necessary upgrades here at *Stone River Village*. Since many of our residents are away over the holidays, visiting relatives, we have scheduled repairs to the Recreation Center and swimming pool for December and January."

Franklin was close to tears as he crumpled his printout of the ideal schedule for Christmas guests. Denise stepped up to comfort him, and to offer an idea. "Remember our tour plan for the RV guests? We have a golf course here, and a nearby shopping center, and lots of close tourist sites."

Brightening up, Franklin got on board. "You're right, sweetheart! We can take everyone to a picnic next to the Recreation Center, then drive to the *Sunny Side Shopping Center* just outside the Village. That would be a fun outing." And as he hugged Denise, he whispered in her ear, "I'm so glad I married a genius!"

But this, too, was just the beginning...

Chapter 35 – The guests arrive

A few days before Christmas, 2019, and with the imminent arrival of guests, Franklin decided to assure a good impression as they arrive, so he opened the garage door to get the lawn mower. As he began mowing, Denise looked at her watch. "Oh, Franklin, hurry! Our first guests should be arriving any minute." He picked up the speed and pace but had barely cut any grass before the first two car-loads of guests arrive. He left the mower in the front yard, as he directed one of the guest cars into the driveway, and the other to a spot on the curb, in the street.

Denise ran to greet them. "Oh, Cousin Claudia and Bill, welcome to *Retirement Heaven*. I'm so glad you could come." That interaction repeated as several more car-loads of guests arrived, lining the street with cars.

As people gathered at the doorway, Denise served as the concierge. "Franklin, these boxes of gifts go into the hallway closet, and the suitcases go into the 3rd bedroom." Franklin greeted the guests and simultaneously whispered to Denise, "Yes, dear. But which bedroom is #3? The one with the bathroom? Or the one on the left?"

Trying to carry too many suitcases and boxes from the doorway, he dropped the boxes of Christmas gifts, which spilled into the yard. As he tried to pick gifts up, he dropped a suitcase, which he then tripped over as he tried to pick up another Christmas gift. In the process, he managed to step on a couple of wrapped Christmas gifts.

The guests look horrified as their neatly wrapped and probably fragile gift boxes were now slightly crushed into the grass, and things got more chaotic as more cars filled with more guests began to arrive. The street quickly filled up with cars, all parked along the curb – and in front of neighbor houses.

Franklin and the guests eventually made it into the house, with the garage door still open, and the lawn mower still in the yard, and cars parked in the street.

And this, still, was just the beginning...

Chapter 36 – Henreeee!

Three hours later, the group was settling in.

Everyone was seated on living room couches, dining table chairs and ottomans...in silence...as though waiting for a magic curtain to open, and the show to begin. The silence was broken by Denise's unexpected shout, as she started the dishwasher. "*FLUSH*!"

Everyone jumped and looked mystified, and Franklin tried to explain, with motions and half sentences. "Oh, that! Well, you see, in the RV, well, whenever...that is, the water temperature...I know we aren't still in the RV, but...oh, never mind." A few confused glances introduced a new period of silence...which was suddenly broken by another shout. '*Hen-reeeeee!*' could be heard from across the street. One of the older guests looked puzzled, and asked, "What was *that*? It sounds so *familiar*...", and Franklin spoke up. "Oh, Robert Casey lives across the street. He played *Henry Aldrich* in the old radio and TV show about..." but he was interrupted by another shout of '*Hen-reeeeee!*' and all the older guests ran out the door toward the house where they could hear '*Hen-reeeee!*' again.

Franklin was looking away from the door and was unaware of the mass exodus of only senior citizens, who were about to deluge Robert Casey with requests for autographs. He continued addressing a half empty room of guests who had no idea what he was talking but, since they weren't even born when the old radio show was on the air.

Continuing, "...about a funny family, and his mother kept calling for her son, '*Hen-reee*!' His wife does that now, for a joke. He retired and moved here to escape the crowds of autograph seekers and I actually promised not to say anything about his being our neighbor. So I hope you will respect..."

Sensing the silence in the room, he stopped and turned to see the almost empty room.

Meanwhile, across the street, Robert Casey and his wife were enjoying a cup of tea in their living room as they heard the doorbell. Robert peeked out through the window. "Oh, no! Not a hoard of autograph seekers!" He motioned to his wife, "Honey, send them away!"

Mrs. Casey opened the door just slightly. The group of older house guests started talking at the same time, acting like a gang of groupies:

Is Robert Casey here?
Are we at the right house?
Could we get an autographed picture?
Would he sign my notebook?

Mrs. Casey closed the door with, "I'm sorry, he's not able to see anyone now. I'm sorry."

The group look at each other as though they had just lost at the weekly bingo game, and they slowly returned to Great's house, mumbling their disappointment.

As they were leaving, Robert mumbled himself. "Don't ever expect anything *good* from someone named *Great!*"

Chapter 37 – Back at the ranch

The gang of groupies made their way back to the Great's living room, and they sat there frustrated and angry – the older guests because of the Robert Casey missed opportunity, the younger ones because they were clueless, and bored. They all looked at Franklin and Denise, as if to say "Well, what's next, in your 'Great' plan?"

Then the silence in the room was interrupted by the sound of a doorbell.

Denise answered the door to see two familiar looking people from the neighborhood, but she couldn't quite place them. "Ah, good evening. Please come in." They entered and moved toward the gathered guests in the living room area.

"I'm Denise, and this is Franklin, and these are our guests for Christmas." After the socially expected nods, "Was there anything in particular you needed?"

"Well, we are here representing the Home Owners Association. I live next door – the house to your right," with a glaring stare toward Franklin. "The one with the yard you evaluated the other day. I trust you received your $200 reward for reporting that my grass was ¼" too high and a showing a very slightly faded green?"

The Christmas guests looked puzzled. But this was just the beginning...

"And *I* live next door in the house on your *left*," looking directly at Franklin. "The one with the yard you also evaluated the other day. I trust you received your *extra* $200 reward for reporting that *my* grass was the same?"

Some mumbling began among the Christmas guests. Now they joined in the stare at Franklin, with a look of shock.

"As we said, we are here representing the HOA. Here are your notices of HOA violations for having six cars parked on the street in front of six houses not your own. That means six $100 fines. And for leaving your garage door open and unattended, another $100 fine."

Franklin's face could be observed as he apparently was adding up the numbers. "Oh, but there is *more,* for leaving your lawn mower in the yard, unattended, another $100 fine. And, oh my, still another, for having a 2x6 foot strip of unevenly mowed lawn, another $100 fine. Let's see ... that adds up to ... $900. Payable to the HOA."

The Great's guests watched the neighbor hand Franklin the bill, and Denise looked as humiliated as the guests looked irritated.

Nodding a 'good-bye' to the group as they walked toward the door, one of the neighbors turned to say, "Oh...Merry Christmas."

After a 30 second silence which seemed like five minutes, Franklin tried to regain some sense of dignity, standing straight and looking at his watch. "Oh, my. It's time to begin preparations for dinner. And by-the-way, we have a *very special menu* tonight," as he attempted to make a timely but obviously un-funny joke, "thanks to my HOA rewards – all meant for *you*, of course, because I spared *no expense* on tonight's meal!"

No one laughed or even smiled, as they joined in to help Denise with dinner, leaving Franklin alone and excluded.

Somehow, he needed to re-establish his role as host.

And that was, still, just the beginning...

Chapter 38 – The recipe for holiday memories

An hour later, the open-room design of kitchen/dining room/living room area was filled with young and old, with younger children playing a board game at the dining room table, a group of teenagers working on a puzzle on the living room coffee table, and another group of young and old guests helping prepare dinner in the kitchen.

But Franklin was nowhere to be seen. He was alone in the master bedroom, hiding his embarrassment and calculating his next move as Christmas Host and Chief Entertainer for the gathered guests. He was also missing out on the usual chaos of a large family preparing a multi-dish extravaganza of a meal, including the expected events that make for funny memories people hold onto forever, including...

The narrow aisle between the kitchen island and the cooking area (stove, oven, microwave and sink) was continuously crowded with younger children perceiving the small space filled with many legs as fun obstacle course. They were endlessly chasing each other around the island, resulting in seniors endlessly grabbing onto anything to prevent a fall. And of course, there was the occasional collision resulting in a bowl of – something – flying through the air like a football into the hands of multiple rookie receivers.

In addition, the oven settings were constantly being changed by a passer-by who thought it wasn't set correctly, or the timing was thrown off by so many hungry and curious guests opening the oven door to check on dinner's progress.

In short, the kitchen was filled with the laughter that creates the savory memories every family has of holiday gatherings and the stuff of stories to be shared every year.

But what was to follow was a memory the entire family and friends would most likely not savor but still remember.

Because, this, still, was ... just the beginning...

But for now, all was well. Franklin had emerged from his short-term isolation, and the events of earlier that day seemed forgotten. Several hours later, the dinner survivors were slowly but not silently washing up the massive stack of dirty dishes. Already, they were laughing about the meal and its effort, which had paid off. All were pleasantly stuffed and ready for a nap.

Chapter 39 – A new plan emerges

Later that night, all were tucked away into their assigned bedrooms, including Franklin and Denise. Franklin prepared for his usual late-night shower. Dressed in a robe and carrying a towel, he walked toward their adjacent, private bathroom, only to find three people in line. Embarrassed and confused, he returned to the bedroom to ask Denise, "What's going on here?"

"Oh, Franklin, it's simple. Since we don't have enough bathrooms for everyone, I assigned them to the ones we have."

Still in need of a shower, Franklin walked out through the living room only to see a line for the bathroom for guest room #1. He then looked into to a hallway to see a line for the bathroom for guest room #2, and finally he saw similar lines for the bathrooms in guest rooms #3 and #4. His journey took him into the kitchen, where he sat at the breakfast nook table, with a discouraged look of resignation.

While sitting there, he saw the HOA "Welcome Kit" brochure on the coffee table, bemoaning its arrival. But this sighting changed everything.

As he perused it, a look of *'I've got it'* came over his face, and he returned to his bedroom, with brochure in hand, to find Denise.

"Denise, I've got it figured out!"

"The bathroom assignments?"

"No. The *car* problem -- and the tour schedule. You know we have to move the cars in the morning before we get another fine. Well, we can move them to the Recreation Center parking lot. It will be empty, since the Center is closed. According to the HOA rules, that's a legitimate parking area for guests. Then, we can rent golf carts for everyone for a caravan to the *Shopping Center*. And, *here's* the genius part -- they can all park their golf carts in the street at the house!" Holding up the HOA brochure, "There are <u>no</u> rules against parking <u>golf carts</u> in the street. I checked!"

Hugging Franklin, Denise whispered, "I'm so glad I married a genius!"

Chapter 40 – The Bocce ball botch

The next day, close to noon, Franklin gathered his guests on the front lawn of his *Stone River Village* home. Acting as the director for the day's activity, he made a formal announcement. "OK, everyone. Just so we're clear, make sure you have your lunch items packed in your cars. The caravan to the Recreation Center for our picnic will begin shortly."

As instructed, though skeptical of the adventure ahead, the guests loaded their cars with wicker baskets of picnic lunches, and double checked both the items and an accurate people-count for each vehicle. After seeing that everyone was ready, Franklin got into his car to lead the caravan, which quickly arrived at the empty parking lot in front of the closed Recreation Center. Franklin and Denise both directed traffic to be sure that all the cars were parked in the designated area for "Guest Parking".

Franklin was behaving like a Keystone Traffic Cop, or perhaps a school crossing guard, waving his arms and pointing as he guided each car into the proper parking spaces. One guest, still in her car, voiced her frustration to a passenger, "Does he think I've never driven or parked a car before? Good grief! How many more days are we visiting here?"

After all the cars were properly parked, the group unloaded their lunch baskets and walked to an adjacent picnic area, only feet away from the cars, with tables, benches and a Bocce ball court, and they began to settle in for lunch. Franklin continued to be the extraverted guide, looking more and more like a middle school teacher's aide, prompting a comment from another guest, "Does he think we couldn't find the picnic tables, right next to the parking lot? Good grief! What day does our flight leave?"

After lunch, one of the eternally optimistic guests offered a compliment. "That was a great picnic lunch, Franklin," even though each guest had prepared and packed their own basket. But the comment was followed by an under-the-breath whisper, "At least there wasn't a car crash on the way!" A quick response came from someone nearby, "The day isn't over yet, dear…"

Soon it was time for the after-lunch agenda -- a Bocce Ball tournament, and, of course, Franklin was the event coordinator, assigning teams. "Franklin, are you good at this game?" asked a guest. Trying to act humble, he answered, "Well, I was the captain of our college team." This got some puzzled looks from even the non-sports folk. "A college Bocce Ball Team?" Nonetheless, Franklin continued, "But I don't want to show off. I'll just watch."

Not realizing the joke, one guest spoke up, "Oh, no Franklin, I want you on *our* team. Let's begin!"

The game began with a round of bowls, and Franklin wasn't doing well. He thought of a plan to change that. Borrowing a relative's cane to pretend to measure how far his ball was from another, he sneakily nudged it into a better position, thinking no one was watching closely enough. But someone *did* notice. "Hey, Franklin, what are you…"

Realizing he had been caught, he had to act quickly. Interrupting the comment by looking at his watch and shifting the focus, he announced, "Oh, by golly! We need to head over to the golf cart rental shop before it closes."

"Golf cart rental?" was heard from more than one person. "Yes, we have to leave the cars here for a fun adventure – a caravan of golf carts to the *Sunny Side Shopping Center*, nearby. They have all kinds of interesting businesses, including antique stores and gift shops with locally made crafts. You'll love it!"

Another optimist in the crowd spoke up. "Oh, thank goodness. I still have a few Christmas presents to buy!" And Franklin, feeling like he had finally hit a home run, looked glib and leader-like, and directed the group to the golf cart rental shop, adjacent to the parking area.

Chapter 41 – The golf cart parade

For some, handling a golf cart was like riding a bike; once learned, it was never forgotten, especially for the golfers in the group. Nevertheless, the scene at the rental office was somewhere along a continuum of smooth to comedic to chaotic. Setting aside the 'smooth', those who were long-time golfers, there were the 'comedic' events, including those who had to sit in threes in the front, and especially those sitting where the golf clubs were normally loaded, and the 'chaotic' struggles by those who had never managed a vehicle with no brakes, nearly crashing into other carts.

"Franklin, I've never driven one of these things. How does this work?"

Answering like an expert, "Well, it's easy. It's electric, and all you do is press down on the accelerator pedal to move, and then remove your foot to stop." The group spent nearly a half hour practicing in the parking lot, driving in circles with jerky starts and stops and nearby misses ... and even some hits.

After a time of "bumper car" antics, Franklin finally got the group organized and into a caravan line, and the parade began.

The community rules required driving golf carts on the wide walking-paths running parallel to the street. However, given the number of carts in the parade, senior citizens who routinely walked that path for exercise were caught off guard by repeated but unpredictable golf cart starts and stops; without car-like breaks, there was no slowing down or speeding up, only "on or off". This made for a constant battle for the "right of way." While there were occasional 'near crashes', and some walkers were seen diving into bushes to avoid being hit, fortunately, there were zero injuries, but that likely could not have been said for complaints to the HOA.

Finally, they reached a sign for *Sunny Side Shopping Center,* and the group of carts entered their parking lot. Again, Franklin directed traffic, which again brought repeated mumblings by cart drivers.

It was now Denise's turn to be the tour guide. "Whew, we made it! Congratulations!" And she added, as much to convince herself as the others, "Now, wasn't that fun, after all?" The question brought a defining silence, but Denise bravely continued. "The antique shops are down *that* row of stores. And the local craft shops are down *that* way."

And as though a bolt of electricity had been sent into the tour, like the starting of the golf carts, everyone scurried about in search of bargains and interesting discoveries.

About two hours later, the even more overloaded caravan of golf carts had taken on additional passengers of boxes and bags, with many in the laps of already uncomfortable passengers and some tied to the canopy over each cart. The guests' appearances had changed from two hours ago, with the excitement of the start of a road race, to the look of exhaustion at the finish line. And the caravan began its return journey to the Great's home.

Until...

One by one, the golf carts suddenly lost speed before reaching the Village. Every cart had a dead battery. Franklin had not calculated the mileage per charge, and the guests were now approaching their own "happiness per mile" limit.

Comments came from the front, middle and back of the line. "What's wrong with these carts?" "The batteries must be dead." "They're all out of power." "Do we have to walk all the way home?"

With multiple stares toward Franklin, the caravan director, he reached for his cell to make a call.

Chapter 42 – The homecoming

Three hours later...after finding out the golf cart
rental office was closed, as was the HOA office,
and tracking down the cell number of the HOA's
chairperson, and then calling for tow trucks, four
flat-bed trucks were blocking the street in front of
the Great's home, causing more phone calls to the
HOA from neighbors.

The guests were still packed inside the carts atop
the flat-beds, looking more exhausted than anyone
at the finish line of a marathon. Some neighbors had
gathered to enjoy the entertainment, reveling in
revenge, and one had called the local police. Two
squad cars arrived with enough officers to begin to
hand out citations for various violations to nearly
everyone. All the tickets found their way to
Franklin.

As the guests climbed out of their golf carts, the
mini-vehicles were unloaded and lined up along the
street. The truck drivers handed Franklin a bill
before driving away and the guests filed past
Franklin, some offering predictable stares and some
avoiding any eye contact at all.

Franklin spent the rest of the night connecting a
battery charger to each cart, one by one, so they
could be driven back to the Recreation Center
parking lot, where all the cars were. The four truck

drivers had insisted on bringing them to the house, in part to verify the address for a "do not respond to any calls from this house" entry into their logs.

The house was a quiet place for the rest of that night.

Chapter 43 – In spite of it all, Christmas arrives

Refusing to surrender, Franklin devised yet another effort to revive the atmosphere. He spent the day designing a special display of Christmas lights for the roof, renting ladders and buying extra extension cords.

At lunch he gathered a select group of "volunteers" to assist with installing a very elaborate array of horizontal and vertical and even elevated lights, which took several hours (and a few near-falls) to complete. The design called for five sets of colorful lights, each 100 feet long. That afternoon he announced a "lighting party" to gather at dusk for an official "*Lights on to Christmas*" spectacle.

At the designated time, just after nightfall, everyone gathered, some happily, some reluctantly, on the front lawn. Franklin began the ceremony, "I know that yesterday ended up on a sour note, but **this** will make up for everything. This home -- *our* home -- with all its warmth and love, is going to light up the entire *Village* with a glow of hope, never before seen in… in this whole… village."

He then flipped a switch and the glare lit up the entire street. Not surprisingly, it also lit up the mixed attention of all the neighbors.

Within ten minutes, a car drove up to the front lawn to deliver a message in a special envelope ... from the HOA. Franklin hesitantly opened it and read its contents aloud:

Dear Mr. and Mrs. Great –

This is a reminder that the HOA has strict rules about…

1. Limits of lights for the holidays (the limit is 50 feet of stringed lights)

2. Limits of how many non-resident guests can occupy a residence at any one time (the Limit is 12)

After a period of silence, everyone but Franklin went back inside. He stayed, also in silence, holding a tape measure as he climbed a ladder to dismantle the lights.

Chapter 46 – An old Christmas tradition finds a new home

It was now Christmas Eve, and time for the tree to be at center stage.

An artificial Christmas tree had been stored in the garage when Franklin and Denise originally moved into their new home, awaiting its grand entrance into the living room. It was the kind of tree that came with its own decorations and lights but with spaces for additional decorations. The tree was in two sections, each removable and neither permanently connected. A group of guests were trying to move it from the garage into the living room, with, of course, Franklin directing the event, with expected difficulties.

It was too wide to be carried through the door horizontally and when carried vertically, the segments kept coming apart. And with the lights still attached to a permanent and continuous electrical cord, it was one more thing to trip over. After several attempts by senior citizens from the group, it was decided to organize a team of younger, smaller and more nimble helpers to coordinate the move.

Denise saw this as yet another opening. "Franklin, this reminds me. Do you remember when you and Myra and Daniel and I set up the Christmas tree when they were just little kids?" Franklin ignored the question and intensified his efforts at choreographing the move. Though some add-on ornaments dropped off en route, leaving a trail of the tree's journey, it finally made its way to a prominent corner near the mantle. He stepped back and announced its arrival. "Finally – there it is, in all its glory!"

Soon after this task was completed, Franklin positioned a tripod and home video camera to take a special group video. He organized the gathered family into a camera pose, around a large couch near the tree. Some were standing behind the couch, some sitting on the couch, some in laps, and some on the floor in front of the couch. Franklin stood to make a special announcement.

"Well, I know everyone is tired, and it's been a stressful time, getting ready for tonight, but this –" ... and a pause came, as he began to tear up, "... *this* is the night we have been waiting for, and preparing for, because..."

He was interrupted by the sound of a doorbell.

Denise jumped from her seat, expecting someone. "I'll get it."

She opened the door and stood back so that everyone could see Myra and Daniel, followed by their children, each with a suitcase. Daniel and Myra, the children of Franklin and Denise, were now adults and had been somewhat estranged from the family, so there were a few quite surprised looks from the guests, but Denise welcomed them both with tight hugs and smiles.

"I see your flight was on time, and you picked up the rental car I reserved for you."

Myra answered first, "Yes, Mom. Everything according to plan."

Denise spoke next. "Franklin?"

Surprised and not sure what to say, he did muster a response. "Well…ah…welcome…home." Then after a pause, "I…I guess ... we should talk…"

It was Daniel's turn. "No, Dad. We didn't come to talk – or to argue. We just wanted to share Christmas with you."

"We've missed you, Dad," added Myra. "Now's not the time to *talk*, but to *trust* – in each other's love, and in the important memories we share…as family."

"Especially memories of Christmas!" added Daniel. "Dad, we've always looked up to you, because you loved us enough that you didn't spend as much time trying to *convince* us of any particular belief, as you did trying to *communicate* with us – to keep a bridge open for those awkward conversations we needed to have about growing up … and preparing for life…"

To which Myra quickly added, "…and preparing for *today*. And that's why we're here – to rebuild that bridge."

Franklin reached out and pulled Daniel and Myra into a hug, as Denise joined in.

The rest of the family and guests responded with smiles, tears, and "aaahhs".

After a couple of beats, with an emotional acknowledgment of the moment, Franklin regained his composure and resumed his announcement. "Tonight is Christmas Eve, when peace and hope and love finally arrive in the midst of … occasional chaos."

"So, we are going to repeat a very special family tradition. Please take your seats again." He refocused the camera on its tripod and then moved into the center of its frame. "Is everyone ready? OK." Then after a deep breath, "Just like every Christmas for many years, I'm going to start the camera, then take my position in the group, next to Denise – and Daniel and Myra…" Denise smiled, pleased with the successful arrangement of the visit by Daniel and Myra. "and we will begin this year's 'Christmas memory' video." He turned on the camera, then moved to his designated position in the group, and began the video's introduction, holding a well-worn, old copy of *'Twas the Night Before Christmas*.

Speaking toward the camera, he continued. "We are here on this Christmas Eve, 2019, to repeat a tradition started by my parents...for some of us gathered here, your grandparents or *great* grandparents, Clara and Gordon Great, who began this tradition on their first Christmas Eve together. Tonight we will take turns reading *'Twas the Night Before Christmas* and then we'll sign the back page of this book, signed every year for the past 80 years."

Now, one by one, family members took turns reading a stanza from the traditional story, then passing the book to the next person. Franklin began the reading.

"'Twas the night before Christmas, when all through the house not a creature was stirring, not even a mouse." He handed the book to Denise, next to him. "The stockings were hung by the chimney with care, in hopes that St. Nicholas soon would be there." She passed the book to Daniel, sitting next to *her*.

"The children were nestled all snug in their beds, while visions of sugar plums danced in their heads," and Daniel passed it to Myra, sitting next to *him*.

The next line was read by a cousin, "And mamma in her 'kerchief, and I in my cap, had just settled our brains for a long winter's nap." Then by an old school friend of Denise, "When out on the lawn there arose such a clatter, I sprang to the window to see what was the matter."

The passing of the book continued around the room, as family and guests took their turns.

"Away to the window I flew like a flash, tore open the shutters and threw up the sash. The moon on the breast of the new-fallen snow, gave a lustre of midday to objects below, When what to my wondering eyes did appear, but a miniature sleigh and eight tiny rein-deer. With a little old driver so lively and quick, I knew in a moment he must be St. Nick. More rapid than eagles his coursers they came, and he whistled, and shouted, and called them by name."

And these next lines were always read by children. A special effort was made for young children to read their own lines, sometimes with an adult's help. Not only was this always done with an educational goal in mind, it was also an opportunity for children to participate in some adult traditions even before they could fully understand their full meaning, as a way of "growing into" both tradition and meaning, creating a foundation for forming values and family memories.

"Now, Dasher! Now, Dancer!
Now Prancer and Vixen! On, Comet! On, Cupid!
On, Donner and Blitzen!
To the top of the porch! To the top of the wall!
Now dash away! Dash away! Dash away all!"

And the passing-it-on of both book and memories continued.

"As leaves that before the wild hurricane fly,
when they meet with an obstacle, mount to the sky;
So up to the housetop the coursers they flew
with the sleigh full of toys, and St. Nicholas too—
And then, in a twinkling, I heard on the roof
the prancing and pawing of each little hoof.
As I drew in my head, and was turning around,
down the chimney St. Nicholas came with a bound.
He was dressed all in fur, from his head to his foot,
and his clothes were all tarnished with ashes and soot."

Again, children were invited to read the next lines.

"A bundle of toys he had flung on his back,
and he looked like a peddler just opening his pack."

"His eyes — how they twinkled! His dimples, how merry! His cheeks were like roses, his nose like a cherry!"

And the adults continued.

"His droll little mouth was drawn up like a bow, and the beard on his chin was as white as the snow; The stump of a pipe he held tight in his teeth, and the smoke, it encircled his head like a wreath; He had a broad face and a little round belly that shook when he laughed like a bowl full of jelly. He was chubby and plump, a right jolly old elf, and I laughed when I saw him, in spite of myself; A wink of his eye and a twist of his head soon gave me to know I had nothing to dread; He spoke not a word, but went straight to his work, and filled all the stockings; then turned with a jerk, And laying his finger aside of his nose, and giving a nod, up the chimney he rose; He sprang to his sleigh, to his team gave a whistle, and away they all flew like the down of a thistle."

Then the tradition continued with the final lines being read in unison by the entire group:

"But I heard him exclaim, ere he drove out of sight *Happy Christmas to all, and to all a good night!*"

Christmas had arrived in a bluster of bumbles, but it ended with a night of calm and quiet.

And now, everyone actually looked forward to the next Christmas reunion.

But this cycle, unfortunately, was just the beginning of new and unseen challenges.

Chapter 47 – A new Christmas tradition appears

The calendar introduced a new year, and a new crisis – the Covid Pandemic.

Throughout 2020, Franklin and Dense continued their basic routines, including a daily review of the local newspaper and adding live stream TV news ... and also adding vaccines and safety masks and social distancing and new ways to shop ... and more.

By late fall, the trends were disturbing. Even with some improvement during the spring and summer, new surges came back as the pendulum appeared to swing, with a potential impact on Christmas gatherings. Frequent headlines appeared in all forms of media:

CHRISTMAS CANCELLED and
HOLIDAY SAFETY A CONCERN

"I can't believe it. How could this be happening?" Denise sighed. And Franklin chimed in, "And we just convinced the HOA to grant us special permission for a larger gathering – and a larger display of lights! And none of it will happen!"

"All those traditions, gone. It's going to be very lonely, this year," came the response.

They sat in silence for a few seconds, allowing the reality of 2020's isolation and sadness to sink in. Then Franklin had an idea. "Wait a minute – maybe it won't be so lonely. Let's organize a VIP party!"

"But Franklin, we can't have *parties* now, not with the pandemic."

"I mean, a *digital* party, through that computer program. What is that called? A "VIP Meeting" – *Virtual-in-Person* meetings!"

"Oh, Franklin, that's a great idea! We could invite any number of people since there's no limit! And it would be safe, and no one would have to spend money on travel. And we won't have to spend money feeding everyone!"

They were on a roll. Denise announced their assignments. "I'll start on the invitation list right away. You figure out how to set it up."

The next morning, Franklin and Denise were sitting at opposite ends of the kitchen table, Denise at a laptop, emailing friends and family and creating a check list, Franklin at another laptop looking up "How to conduct your own VIP meeting". His head filled with questions, he called his techie neighbor who had retired from an IT job.

Chapter 48 – A Covid Christmas

The Christmas tree and decorations were all in place as the backdrop for the camera's view and the VIP session had started, with Franklin as the host. While participants were logging in, some could see a small lizard in the background, climbing the Christmas tree. A few minutes later, there was a spark and a poof of smoke from a limb on the tree. Everyone logged on at the time cringed, but since the action was behind Franklin, he thought it was meant for him. He fidgeted and shifted his position, hoping to make a better screen impression, which further puzzled the onlookers.

Managing to re-focus the group's attention, Franklin began the session. "OK, it's time for a very special moment -- our annual Christmas reading of *'Twas the Night Before Christmas*. This is *one* tradition that has **not** been cancelled! I sent everyone their assigned pages, so get out your instructions, as we repeat a tradition that has been in our family, now for *81 years* -- and *still counting!*"

When they reached the last line, the unison reading of *"Happy Christmas to all, and to all a good night,"* Franklin was not the only one with teary eyes. Somehow, they had survived a Covid Christmas. And that required a special toast. "Well, through the years, we've all had special vacations and family reunions, and this one has been among the most memorable. So I'd like to offer a toast -- to past, and future vacations and reunions that will last forever in our minds and hearts. Who knows, perhaps one of you will even write a book, or make a movie about them, but more importantly, we will all keep them alive in our memories."

They all raised a glass -- of wine or juice or water -- as Franklin continued, "Here, here. And even though, this year, we are in different physical places, I know where each and every one of you is, right at this moment: in my mind and in my heart, where you will always be." Franklin and Denise held a hand with a firm grip and lovingly looked to each other. Then they embraced and kissed, on screen. Which received this response:

"Aaahhhh…"

But as their "PDA" (public display of affection) slightly intensified to a more sensual kiss and hug for more than a few seconds, each person had a different comment, but all shared simultaneously,

"Eeewh! Grandpa! Dad! Grandma! Mom! Eeewh!"

Gathering his composure, Franklin continued, with gravitas. "I have an idea. Let's all, silently, go out to our individual front yards, to, *together*, look up to the sky, to see the *Christmas Star* – something not seen for hundreds of years – a visible sign of hope for a new, and better year!"

This would be a great ending to a great story, but still, it was just the beginning...

Chapter 49 – A pattern emerges

It was now the summer of 2021 and Covid vaccines were getting more common and Franklin and Denise had arrived at a local clinic to better their chances for handling the pandemic. "Good morning. I'm Franklin Great, and this is my wife, Denise. We have an appointment for our vaccines."

"Oh, Good morning. Yes, I see your names on our list. Right this way."

They walked down a hallway and entered a lab as another nurse was drawing the vaccine into a syringe. Franklin took one look at the needle -- and fainted, just thinking about it.

-   -   -

Later, in the fall, as pandemic-life was now becoming a new-normal, they were engaged in their morning routine when Denise observed, "You know Franklin, now that the vaccine seems to be a success, I think we could invite some guests for another family Christmas reunion. What do you think?"

He fainted, just thinking about it.

-   -   -

Still, time marched on, and it was now Summer, 2022. Franklin was entering the same medical building but wearing a new T-shirt with a huge syringe in the center, with vertical letters to its left spelling "EVEN" and vertical letters to its right spelling "ODD."

"Good morning. I'm Franklin Great, and this is my wife, Denise. We have an appointment for our vaccines."

"Good morning. Yes, I see your names on our list. But, what does the "odd" and "even" mean?"

"Oh, it's a reminder that I get the boosters # 1, 3, 5, and 7 in the right arm, and boosters # 2, 4, and 6 in the left arm."

With an expression indicating the need to be prepared for an unusual experience, and a nod to a nearby orderly, she drew the syringe.

And Franklin fainted, just thinking about it.

Made in the USA
Middletown, DE
05 November 2022